KGEBETLI MOELE

Room 207

Kwela Books

This publication was supported by
the National Arts Council of South Africa.

NATIONAL ARTS COUNCIL
OF SOUTH AFRICA

Published by Kwela Books,
a division of NB Publishers (Pty) Limited,
40 Heerengracht, Cape Town, South Africa
PO Box 6525, Roggebaai, 8012, South Africa

Cover image by Guy Tillim
Cover design by Michiel Botha at Flame Design
Typography by Nazli Jacobs
Set in Stone
Printed and bound by Paarl Print,
Oosterland Street, Paarl, South Africa

First edition, first impression 2006
ISBN-10: 0-7957-0234-5
ISBN-13: 978-0-7957-0234-1

To Nare,

who lost his mind and his dreams –

you are still loved

"All men dream: but not equally. Those who dream by night in the dusty recesses of their minds wake in the day to find that it was vanity: but the dreamers of the day are dangerous men, for they may act their dream with open eyes, to make it possible. This I did."

T. E. LAWRENCE, Seven Pillars of Wisdom

Contents

Refuge

———

207

It used to be a hotel, back in the days of . . . you know, those days which the rulers of this land don't want you to forget. Corner of Van der Merwe and Claim, there used to be a hotel. Once. Then. And now it's a residential. I stay there in room 207. We stay there, although we don't really say we stay there: it's been a temporary setting, since and until . . . I can't tell. What I do know is that we have spent eleven years not really staying there. Matome always says, "It is our locker room away from home, baba."

This room is our safe haven during the lighted dark night of dream city.

S'busiso (we call him the Zulu-boy and, from this day on, you will call him the Zulu-boy too), Molamo, D'nice, Modishi and, like you heard, Matome, ke mo Molobedu. For us 207 was, and is, our home.

Open the door. You are welcomed by a small passage with a white closet on your left, full of clothes and innumerable handwritten papers that are more valuable to us than our lives. Bags fill the rest of the space and on the top there is a Chinese radio, a very expensive keyboard, a trumpet, two hotplates and about a thousand condoms.

The floor is wooden, giving away the fact that this hotel was built when wood was the in-thing, fashionable. It needs help.

A door on your right leads into the bathroom.

Open the door.

The place is rotting. Some of the tiles have cracked and some have lost their grip entirely and fallen off. The cream-white paint is cracking, showing the old paint underneath and the bad paintwork done over the years. The air is humid and heavy because the small window is rarely opened and, if you do open it, you will lose your soap or maybe your toothpaste.

Before we made the rule about having the window permanently closed, toothbrushes, antiperspirants, body lotions and toothpastes vanished. Until, one day, a kilogram of washing powder vanished and Matome cried because his laundry was still dirty and no one had washed their clothes. From that day on the window was closed for good and for that reason the air is humid and heavy.

On your left is the basin, still in good condition. In front of you the toilet, missing only the toilet lid; it has never seen newspaper, and, in better times, there is always soft toilet paper – the kind the Zulu-boy prefers (that is advertised by small children on our national television). Even in the dark days, and the even darker days that may be to come, I can bet with my balls that we won't use newspaper here, Matome will always steal – unroll the whole toilet roll from a public toilet for the comfort of our delicate butts.

Then there is the bath on your right. The ceramic coating is scratched and has, over the years, fallen victim to its own predators (whatever they are). If you had an appetite for a hot bath you'd lose it, I'm sure of that, and you'd wash in the basin instead.

Right above the back of the bath is the geyser – rusty, leaking, with exposed electric cables. Sometimes I feel sorry in advance for whoever is in the bath the day it decides it has had enough. Though, sometimes, I wish it would happen to me and then I could take the landlord to court and have the out-of-Hillbrow party that Matome says we are going to have the day we move out of Hillbrow for good.

Matome's party doesn't have a set date, since we all came to the dream city in different ways and, indifferently, became united. He's always talking about it though, saying that it will be the greatest party in the history of Hillbrow.

Come in, come in.

This is the study cum dining room cum sitting room, you can sit on this single bed or that double bed, or you can just find a spot and make yourself comfortable anywhere you prefer, even on the floor. Brother, you are home.

This is our home, as you can see for yourself. This, our cum everything room, and that is our kitchen. That is the hotplate. As you can see there's no refrigerator. That, the sink, is always like that. The dishes are washed only when we are about to have our last meal of the day, which, sometimes, is our first meal of the day but the last anyway. After that, we just put the dishes there until the next meal, then we wash and use them and put them there again, but there are no cockroaches here. Believe me, it is a miracle that we don't have them. Go to some flats and they have forty million of them. Wage war, and sweep them away, dead, and they will be there the next day like nothing happened.

We once had a television set, it was old but it was a television. I guess it just got tired of sitting on the table and being a television, everybody looking at it when it suited them, changing the channel without its consent. One day, Modishi was having the darkest of days and hating everything with two legs and a mouth. He looked at it, maybe it asked him: "What are you looking at? I'm not on and I don't want to be; it's my turn to look at you guys."

Maybe that's what it told him because suddenly Modishi just picked it up like it was a weightless thing and threw it out of the balcony door.

The radio: Matome's radio. These Chinese things. It no longer played

15

compact disks and I hate when, in the morning, I'm woken up by the irritating voice of some DJ from dream city's very own youthful radio station. I don't hate YFM at all, but I like to wake up from my sleep very slowly. Those seconds. Those seconds in the morning when my consciousness regains itself. Those seconds when I don't even know my other name, my hopes and dreams, while I'm thinking about my nightmares, sweet or sad, with a smile I only smile for myself – a smile I'm saving for the one that will deserve not only my love but every-thing that it comes with.

Anyway, it woke me, so I opened the radio up. And, since then, it's been fighting for space with the keyboard, the hotplates and those fashionable things called condoms, which our government supplies to us, without charge, for our very own cautious pleasures.

The other citizens, those that we share this 207 haven with, the little mice, are not here now, but don't worry too much because they will be here soon, when the time is right for them to come out. Then maybe you can have a chat with them too. Unlike the rats I kind of have a soft spot for these little mice. They don't eat our clothes, shoes and papers. It's like we have an agreement with them; we respect each other and each other's property.

The only bad thing is that they scare the visiting females. They are so free that they will walk over your head, not intending to offend you in your peaceful sleep but, like you, they are chasing their own sets of dreams in dream city. They don't eat rat poison; Ga le phirime is here but they live with it.

This, as you can see, is the wall of inspiration. To us, to me, they are not role models at all but people just like you and me, who, in their very own ways and byways, made it to the top. We put them up on the wall so that when one of us is down he can look at them, because some of them have lived through this Hillbrow, lived it to get out of it.

You know these faces, that's Boom Shaka. If you had something cold in your hand, something cold that you were drinking when they got on stage, by the time these ladies get off-stage it will be very hot.

How?

I don't know, but I have experienced it.

That's the brother Herman Mashaba. Our very own self-made billionaire. He is one hell of an inspiration, if you allow me to say. Like us all here in 207, except for D'nice, he is a dropout of that great institution of education we call university. University of the North, to be precise. It is a very sad black story and we can all tell it very well.

Herman Mashaba is the green shoot that pushes itself out of the heavy ash to greater heights. Remember, that was back in the days of . . . I take off my hat, my shoes and my balls to this exceptional darkie brother of the soil. To me, he is just pure inspiration. When I'm drowning, I just take a look at this brother and he gives me a hand, pulling me out, and I know everything will be fine. Everything will be all right.

This, the second Jesus: Che.

I hate all politicians, so I hated Mandela the politician, but I loved Mandela the freedom fighter and I miss that Mandela.

Not that I miss the past.

No.

Che was a guerrilla with an AK-47 in his hands. No history needs to absolve Ernesto Guevara de la Serna. "At the risk of sounding ridiculous, let me say that the true revolutionary is guided by feelings of love." He did say that, breathed it and died living it, and I know what you are going to say: What a waste!

17

Greedy.

The wall of inspiration – these brothers are there for their spiritual and soulful support only.

This is the only photo of us, which we had taken in this city at Park Station – Parkie as it is known by the masses. It was Matome's idea as we were walking out of his office. It was taken by one of those camera-men who hang around Parkie to capture one's first moments in this dream city.

These paintings are originals, painted by Molamo, in the rare moments when he gets a painting attack. Then he has to paint his thinking. To me they are just pictures, but every female who comes in here gets caught by this one and they end up wanting it for themselves. To me it's just a picture of a neglected, black baby boy taking his first steps unaided, with eyes that promise the world: "I'm here." I fail to see why the visiting females fuss about it so much.

This one has a place in this heart. This is the African warrior. The Masai warrior. Standing tall and comfortable on one leg. I guess he is looking at . . . Well, he is enjoying whatever he is looking at. It makes him comfortable and at peace. But that too is coming to its sad end, for globalisation is hungry at their door, their resistance is finally crumbling and things are finally falling apart.

Only Molamo's Tebogo finds this one alluring, but even she doesn't want to have it. Look carefully for it is disguised. What you are looking at is not what the painting is about. If you can look carefully in this confusion of a painting, you will see that there is a nude couple with a baby. I was not aware of this fact until Tebogo pointed it out. I wondered why she didn't want it. She gave the reason: she wants to be part of it and she feels it rejects her every time. Then I thought, well, she is too much somehow.

These are Molamo's stickers. This one is a quote from a great man of the soil, Ali Mazrui: *"We are the people of the day before yesterday."*

And this one! I don't think even the Almighty can put this into practice; I always fail before I even start: *"You should have twenty rands that you used the day before yesterday and used yesterday, use it for today and still use it for tomorrow and all the other tomorrows."*

This is our mirror. I have seen things in this mirror; I have seen people lose themselves in front of it. I don't know if it is because it's a big mirror, but come here very early every morning and you'll witness what the mirror on the wall is witness to and reflects.

This is our safe haven here in Hillbrow. I like to call Hillbrow our little mother earth in Africa because here you'll find all races and tribes of the world. Here you'll find Europeans and Asians that by fate have become proud South Africans, taking a long shot or maybe even a short shot at a dream or dreams of their own.

It's dream city and here dreams die each and every second, as each and every second dreams are born. However beyond counting the dreams, they all have one thing in common: money. Respect and worship are the ultimate goals; everybody here is running away from poverty.

Poverty. I have lived too much of it. But what really *is* poverty? Have I really seen too much of it? Lived too much of it? Can you really measure poverty? Can you measure suffering? Can you measure joy?

I once asked a question when we were having a poverty sleep. Matome and D'nice were sharing the double bed with Modishi. I was on the sponge with Molamo and the Zulu-boy was on the single bed. As always, the room was never really dark. I can't really remember what time it was but it was after eleven. We weren't talking much, maybe we were saving energy or maybe we were just mad at ourselves for drinking all the money over the weekend.

The Zulu-boy was and is always the one talking, talking about that day after the out-of-Hillbrow party, when the world will be worshipping us. Talking about that day like he knew the exact date, had peeped into the future and seen it all. Now, he is just killing the time between now and then – describing in detail the convertible that Modishi will be driving up the N1, chasing the African air with Lerato on his left.

This was exactly what we needed at that moment: reassurance that our venture, this dream-venture in dream city, would pay off, eventually.

Modishi smiled privately to himself and so did I, the hunger being consumed by our joy.

Then I asked a question, "If you die of hunger while sleeping tonight and wake up in heaven, what will you say to the big Man?"

I thought they were still thinking of what they would say. But they never answered me. I tried to think of what I would say to Him. My mind got stuck with the same overwhelmed feeling that the general masses get when they meet the celebrated of His green earth.

No one said a word and we drifted off to sleep.

Mortals

Matome

Matome was always the first one to wake up: "People, I'm waking up."

He always said that in a way that would make you think you were responsible; that you were somehow making him sleep against his will.

"People, I'm waking up."

Then he'd slip into some sandals and get himself into the bathroom. He'd open the hot tap and there would be the sound of water filling the bath and being replaced in the geyser, then the flush of the toilet.

I don't know why it was, but every time he got into hot water his manhood felt the warmth and hardened; every time he had a bath he had a full erection with it. But, that was the only place he ever got one – in hot water.

Medium height, dark skin and charming, he had something in him that made all people want to trust him.

I trusted him from the moment I saw him, and we had been together from that first week, in our first year in dream city. Thursday of that same week I moved in with him: I was studying broadcasting and he was doing sound engineering. The next day I had to give him R350, which he was supposed to add to his R350 for the month's groceries. I don't know if he ever did add his money, but when I came back that afternoon there was a party at my place (as he put it). It was my flat party, the first of the many something parties that I was to party in this city.

I was very surprised. I was overwhelmed that so many people came to enjoy a flat party for me. I drank and got drunk.

The next morning he woke me up, saying, "We are going to buy groceries now. I'm not your wife."

We got to the friendly supermarket and he had a friendly talk with the security guards, like he knew them from long ago. Then he asked to have a friendly one-to-one with the manager, but he wasn't there, so he took a trolley, put some plastic bags in it and we proceeded.

"Do you like this?" he asked.

"Do we need that?" I answered.

But he ignored me and said, "Well, do you like it? I don't have all day."

He took everything he wanted without even considering its price. When we got to the till he started packing the groceries into the plastic bags right in front of the cashier.

"Are you paying for this?" I asked.

He looked at me and said, "Where do you think I'd get the money from? I'm not working and we drank all your money yesterday."

I just walked out, leaving him there. I wasn't scared. I was angry. How could he be so irresponsible with my money and expect to walk into the supermarket, charm the security guards, and then take whatever he wanted and walk out? But that's exactly what he did, the security guards helping him with the bags. Matome smiling like he was walking down a red carpet. The groceries must have cost R900 or more and that was without the meat that came from the butchery.

"You want to pay for everything? If you have the money, pay, but I will take. I don't like taking, but if you ask, you won't have," he said, looking at me with burning eyes, dead serious. "Sometimes you have to do things, bad things, in order to get to a peaceful end."

Matome was a man of all seasons: I took him for a baobab tree, the tree that decided one night that it was going to be different from all trees and swapped itself upside down, so that, unlike all the other trees, its photosynthesis took place underground, right next to the water.

People believe in things. Some people believe in God. Others believe in money. Matome was a person who believed in himself. It was like he gave birth to himself. He never, in all the years that we lived together, mentioned anything of his past. Whenever the conversation got to the point where he would have to tell someone something about his past, he would say, "We are here now, forget the past, and think about now, today and tomorrow, which is where we are going. You can only say sorry about the past, and it doesn't matter whether you are sorry or not. It has passed."

Matome's past was a closed case. He would listen when anybody was telling a story about something from their past and he'd laugh, if it was funny, or be sorry, if it needed that, but he would never tell of anything of his own.

Women always wanted him, they fantasised about him. They would make advances, but he just floated and then, later, he would make one big joke about it, like he didn't care. And, of course, he didn't. We all envied him and the cheese boys wanted to befriend him, but he was everyone's friend whatever your background was. As he put it: "Your background is your background; it's yours, I don't care about it. I only care about the eyes, the soul, the human being, the face."

He had many friends. Everybody was his friend. In his world the term 'stranger' was nonexistent, but just because everybody was a friend to him did not mean that he didn't have enemies. He had a trainload of them, all in third class, and most of them were of the female species. Only because they loved him at first, and even slept in the same bed with him for a couple of nights, but then quickly discovered that to Matome love was not about sex. And then they hated him for that. And some even made allegations of this and that.

Like that beautiful girl Debra. God knows, I wished she was making all those advances at me.

One night we were having a party and the war against Isando was not going to end very soon thanks to Matome's charm. Some of our guests were already lost to the war and one of them had already thrown up.

Debra, as one of my uncles always observed of most of the girls who grew up in Mamelodi, was a true lelaenara, and that night she proved him very right. She was standing just in front of her boyfriend, stroking him with her soft hands. Standing there, she called to Matome and said, out loud for everyone who could hear to hear, "Since the day I first saw you I have always wanted to fuck you."

Excuse the language, but that's exactly what came out of her mouth.

She continued, "And you are always fucking running away, what's wrong with you? This guy!" She was preaching now. "I want to give it to him for free, but he doesn't fucking want it. Others have to sweat for it, but I'm giving it to you for free. Free!"

Her eyes were pleading, and Matome, who rose to every occasion, smiled, stroked his manhood and said, "This one, sweetie, you won't have to sweat for it, you'll have to die for it. You'll have to fucking die for this one, sweetie."

Matome danced on and she concluded, "I'm going to fucking rape you one of these days."

She turned back to her boyfriend, with an innocent-guilty smile and a shake of the head, as if she didn't know that he was there, and said, "I was just playing."

Matome had love for the female species. He had nothing but love and tender care. And he made them all happy, made them laugh until they complained about having headaches and God knows what else he made them feel. Matome loved them, but not the way you and I will tenderly love those members of the female species. He had innumerable girlfriends, one after the other, and the same thing always happened. From Matome all they got was love and no sex. One of them asked me once, after sleeping with, and being loved by Matome for about a month or so, she asked, "What kind of a man is Matome?"

Dimakatso was what they called her and, true, she was all that and more. From a township called Ikageng in Potchefstroom, she was here in the city making a dream come true.

Mind you, it was a fair question, because I was right there too; my bed was just a metre and a half from his. We would talk and they'd play puppy-love-play and, finally, thinking bad thoughts, I'd drift off into a very sweet sleep. But, how could I answer that kind of a question, because clearly the question had implications. The real question was obviously: Why is it that Matome doesn't have it with me? Does he have a problem with his thing or is it me?

"What do you think?" was the logical thing that came out of my big mouth and with that I invited no further questions, and then I felt sorry about shutting her down, so I said, "He is your man, you tell me."

Then she smiled and shook her head, not knowing what to tell me. I reached out and touched her. I could feel her heart beating faster, the pulse increasing, and the sorry-sadness drifting away. She smiled a smile that said I should not stop, so I did what I do, believing it was for the best.

"Tell me the difference between love and sex?" Matome asked her a long time afterwards.

She looked at him, trying to come up with a quick answer, an answer that wasn't there, and so he told her, "Sweetie, love is a process, sex is an act. Sex ends, but love doesn't end."

"I never thought of it that way," she responded, and Matome told her, "Don't think, I'm giving you the facts here! I love you and I want you. If I'm not having sex with you, it doesn't mean that I don't love you. And it doesn't mean I can't have sex with you, it's just that I don't want to have sex. I want to be loved, but I don't want to have sex at this time in my life."

Dimakatso looked at Matome as if trying to connect this statement with Matome and her understanding of him, but it was as if she didn't want to be in the state of understanding which Matome had reached.

"Remember, sex is an act but love is a process. Do you understand me?"

And she said, "Yes."

And with that I got myself a girlfriend. First Dimakatso was Matome's and then she was mine and we were still living in the same room.

"Remember, love is a process, to be cared for and understood at all times," Matome told her, but throughout his search for a companion, one who understood love at his level, he never found one.

It was just unfortunate, the Dimakatso thing, but then another name for sex is making love and there's not much difference between making love and sex to you and me, I think.

"I can go out now and buy sex. What they are selling is an act that ends; even between two people, who love each other very much, it, sex, still remains an act: it ends. It is never love, as it has nothing to do with love," Matome concluded.

Smile, sweetie, it will be all right.

That was the way Matome always wanted them, smiling, happy. He could keep everybody smiling; after all, he was always smiling, even in the darkest of times.

Even when he lost his mother, he smiled as always, like nothing really happened, throughout the whole week. On Thursday, we were laughing as always, having one of those connections when I wished he was my blood brother, and it was then that he asked me to go with him to his home in Bolobedu. I agreed; we were writing an exam the following morning at nine o'clock and after that, we would leave the city.

He said nothing until we got to Bolobedu, where, to my surprise, I found out that we were there to bury his mother. I felt sorry and angry. I never knew he had just lost his mother. I felt sorry for him, which was, of course, the reason why he hadn't told me. He knew that if he had told me I would act sad, and he hated it when people did that.

That day Matome wasn't sad, it was like he was happy that she had died. I asked him if he loved his mother and he said, smiling, "The day you die is better than the day you were born." Without any remorse but with conviction.

But there are things in our world that will touch your heart no matter how you try to avoid them. There are things that can shake an unshakeable heart, squeeze it so hard that the pretence of happiness fails and crumbles.

A few days later, I got back to the flat and discovered that Justice was having a bath – the whole flat smelled of him. Justice was the homeless man who lived around the corner.

I laughed at first, not laughing because there was anything funny, but in admiration of Matome, the Jesus-ness in him. Then he started apologising and, as my girlfriend was with me, I did not know what to say.

We always passed Justice in his corner. Sometimes I would talk to him or Matome would have something for him, but most of the time we just passed him by.

"I could not pass him today," Matome said, innocently.

He gave him some of his clothes and food, then he shared his bed with him. My friend and I didn't sleep a wink; you know how the female species are.

He stayed with us for four days and nights, then he disappeared out of our lives just like that and we never saw him again. We left him in our home and, when we returned, he wasn't there and the door wasn't locked. The clothes that we had given him were washed, hanging on the makeshift washing line in the bathroom, but he was gone.

On the bed we found a piece of paper with a cartooned face of Justice, smiling and happy, and underneath a caption that read: *I have met two people in my life and they made it meaningful.*

Justice was from up north. He came to dream city to make his dreams come true. You don't have to ask what happened, just draw a conclusion for yourself; but there are people like Matome, who don't want to talk a bit about themselves but love to listen to others.

Justice's father had been a successful businessman, but he had lost his dear mother and father in a car accident the very same day he turned twenty-one. They had been driving back after celebrating the important day with their son.

With that he inherited everything.

When he was eighteen he had come to dream city to further his education, but Justice failed the first year and the second one and then the third. He had a car when he came here and a flat, with a washerwoman who came every day. He had a billion friends and saw the underwear of almost all the girls who were going to Wits.

"If you ever meet anyone that was a student at Wits in those years, ask them: 'Do you know Ice?'" Justice said, smiling, thinking of those days that are gone and never coming back. They called him Ice in those wonderland days of his.

It took him three years, some expensive sports cars, which were written off, some expensive fashion, some travelling around this God's green earth, a hundred thousand rands' worth of drugs and alcohol, an innumerable number of orgasms, and then, finally, it was all gone, together with his mind.

"How much money?"

"Enough."

"How much is enough?"

"Four point two."

He was talking to Matome. There was a pause as Matome calculated the what ifs, giving away a smile with the thought of every what if . . .

"You were young?"

Then silence, as the truth fell on us that maybe we wouldn't be alive if we were in his shoes. Then Matome said, "But didn't you think of anything that would keep you off the streets?"

Justice kept silent for a moment and looked at Matome, as if he wanted to see his soul first. Then he smiled, like he had seen Matome's soul, and, now he had seen it, it would understand.

"Ntepa." He said it hard, and paused as if he disapproved. "Ntepa." He said it again, this time a little softer, as if there was nothing better. "Ntepa," he concluded in a lower tone, a deep voice that sounded like he had given in, had surrendered to it and it had taken him prisoner.

"Ntepa is a worthless, useless, shitty thing." He said it again like the first time: hard, with anger. "No, I'm lying. It is a very powerful thing that needs to be respected, and if you disrespect it . . ."

He looked at himself from the chest down to Matome's old shoes and then up into Matome's eyes.

Flip the page.

On the other side he had drawn Matome, me and an exact replica of my girlfriend – with all her beauty enhanced and emboldened. She was the only one that he had drawn from head to toe. Matome and I were only half-bodies. My hand was stroking my girlfriend, but despite that I didn't look happy. Matome was drawn with his permanent smile. Underneath, the caption read: *Life is treacherous quicksand with no guarantees . . .*

That was definitely from one of Head's books, but I couldn't remember which one.

I understood the other side, the picture and the message, but I couldn't connect the picture and the message on this side.

That morning was the last time Matome and I saw Justice. A homeless man was the only thing in this life that I ever saw shake Matome's heart. And the cruel part of it was that there was nothing he could do about it. Justice was gone.

D'nice

Honestly, we are a drinking nation. We don't go, during the holidays, on tours of this lovely country of ours, from the Klein Karoo to Skukuza, via Borakalalo National Park. No.

Why not?

Because we don't care. That's for white people. I don't blame them. Don't blame us. We drink, grill meat and cook some hard porridge, then quarrel and maybe end up fighting or trying to stop one fight from getting way out of hand.

I was at a New Year celebration; it was just before half-four, New Year. Only a few people, the real party animals and drinkers, were still partying and drinking. Matome and I were still fighting the war, which so far had been without incident, and then these two guys who were sitting not far from us, sharing a beer, started to quarrel about something. We didn't take any notice of them and they quarrelled on, still sharing the beer.

The first guy said, "You take me as the things you shit in the toilet."

The second guy, ignoring him, said, "Let me smoke."

And the first guy took a cigarette out of his pocket and gave it to him, repeating to him, as he gave him the cigarette, "You take me for your shit in the toilet."

He even gave him the lighter.

Then the second guy, after lighting the cigarette, replied, "If you feel like you are someone else's shit in the toilet, then you are shit."

"Joe! Joe! Joe! I'm going to break you, going to break you now."

"Hey! Drink beer. This is the first day of this year. So don't try, because then I'll have to do something very bad to you. It will be a bad year for you."

They went on talking, frightening and threatening each other with harmless words. To make it seem even more harmless they were sharing the cigarette and a seven-fifty lengolongolo.

Surprise.

It got very ugly and there was blood everywhere.

Afterwards, they patched it up with each other, and shared a cigarette and a lekhamba, like they didn't want to break each other's heads any more. And that was how I met D'nice for the first time; after he had been fighting with his dear friend.

D'nice came to the city the very same year that I met Matome. He came, as everybody who comes to dream city, hoping and dreaming. He came to the city to continue with his education. He was brilliant, with a three digit IQ. He'd passed eight of the nine subjects in matric with straight As and got a B in the other one – and that's way ahead of the fifteen points needed to gain acceptance to Wits.

Well, let's look carefully at the issues.

The issue here: The cost of tertiary education and black students.

We were all like D'nice in one way or another, or maybe like him in every way.

Your mother works as a washerwoman. Your father, at fifty-one, is on the blue card, leaving his house every morning to take refuge and comfort with his mates in the war against alcohol. If you're lucky you have a grandparent or two and through them some pension money, which doesn't really help with anything, but is better than nothing. Then there are seven of you. Your two older sisters, who are sitting at home with one-year computer certificates waiting for that job, which, let's be honest, isn't coming. But what is coming is a child, whose father won't show up, even at its first birthday party. The other two are doing grade twelve this year, and the others are in grade ten and grade eight respectively.

Then you get admitted to the great institution and, before even three months have passed, the last cent from the blue card is gone.

Have you ever been at university?

With two pairs of black shoes (the good pair and the other pair, in which your feet act as the sole – thank God your toes are still intact), two T-shirts, two round-neck skippers, one V-neck, one vest, two pairs of underwear (that should be written off), four pairs of jeans and four pairs of smart trousers. Not to forget about the pair of washed-every-evening socks. You have absolutely no pocket money at all, and then there is the institution itself, which keeps reminding you that you need to pay your fees or you are out. As if you weren't their student at all, but were working. Four months pass with their share of peer pressure and stress. Then comes the student awards and they award you the most unfashionable student of the year or, worse still, they look at you as some kind of socially handicapped library-dweller . . .

It gets too deep inside, into the soul, and then you start to lose a kilogram every two and a quarter days and now your well-cared-for clothing hangs on you like it was never yours.

Have you ever been at a tertiary institution of education and witnessed what the black students are going through?

D'nice survived Wits by his own will and sometimes, when he looked back and thought about how he made it, it puzzled him.

From a high school in the rural areas, where not that much matters much and the school didn't even have a proper office. From a place where what matters the most is to see a smile on your face.

He came into the heart of the dream city with his dreams, putting on a smile with a promise: I am going to show them the best of me and they will think I'm from a private school.

Three months into the thing, peer pressure ran him down, and he realised nobody gave a shit about the smile on his face.

He lay on his bed in his paid-for room, courtesy of his scholarship, thinking that he was in the wrong place, thinking that he didn't belong there, while the tears were trying hard to wet the bed.

Then he made a decision.

He got up, wiping away the tears, shook his head and promised them, "They have to take me as I am, because I am what I am."

And that was that.

D'nice was the kind of guy who'd wake up at ten to prepare an assignment that was due at four. He had no need for a rubber or Tipp-Ex. He wrote. It was written. No looking back. His was always the last assignment in the box. He was never known to attend more than three lectures a week.

He was called to the dean's office once and, like always, he was drunk. The dean gave him a tongue-lashing and D'nice took it calmly, and when the dean was tired, he looked at him calmly. The dean knew that D'nice was always in the A-plus category on every exam and assignment and, to make it even worse, he came from a rural public school.

D'nice said, "Sir, I have a very different mind, which I don't really understand myself. I get very bored and it wanders, then I have to keep it forever in a state of intoxication to control it."

He said that to the dean and that became D'nice's passport for part-time studying and permanent intoxication – a definite, sure way to be survived by the great institution.

D'nice was not your average genius with spectacles. He looked more like a conservative man with short hair and because of that you would miss the fact that he was a genius. He would read a paragraph in the paper and then he would know it, and you could do that too, but you can't rewrite it in the same way it was written, can you? He could do that and he wouldn't even miss a comma. He read everything once, and if he reread it, it was giving him some kind of philosophical problem.

Long ago, when he was still doing his matric, the mathematics teacher wrote a problem on the board and said, "Who can tell me the answer to this sum?"

D'nice wasn't interested, he didn't even hear the question because he was busy at the back of the class with some other thing that interested his mind.

The teacher let a few minutes pass, thinking that perhaps the pupils were still working it out.

"Somebody give me the answer?"

Nobody came with the answer. The pupils weren't working out the answer, they were just waiting for someone to give an answer, any answer. Then the teacher started to shout in anger, and that was when D'nice took notice and told him the answer, but the teacher replied, "I am not interested in the answer but how to get it."

D'nice kicked his chair back and walked to the board. He looked at the others, then wrote the whole sum back to front, starting with the answer first. After he'd finished he put the chalk back in the teacher's hand and sat down again.

Then the puzzled teacher suddenly became aware of what he'd done and was thankful that he hadn't asked D'nice to explain what he'd written on the board, because it would have been embarrassing on his part.

Jeans were never his thing. He always wore smart trousers, black, khaki or brown, very well-ironed, and a T-shirt. His feet were always imprisoned in a pair of shining black formal shoes. He had a pair of sandals, but those were only for walking about in the haven. He also had a pair of sports shoes for when he and Matome would jog to Sandton and back.

You could talk politics, sport, cars, fashion and even your professional work with him, and he'd always have something to say or ask you some puzzling question.

Why?

Because he spent too much of his time in the library, not choosing what to read like you, but reading.

D'nice was poor, had a scholarship, but he was deadly at poking the opposite sex.

His speciality: the rich, spoiled white girls.

He dated Michelle in his final year. Michelle was a final-year music student. It was after he had poked with this member of God's chosen few, and the beauty was resting, that his life changed. He was bored, life bored this man, and his thinking wandered. His eyes were running around, up and down, wishing that the god of Isando would appear and provide that which he provides best. Then his eyes landed on a keyboard. He switched it on and played it like he was born playing it, played it so well that the beauty woke up.

She just looked at him playing and maybe the world stopped and listened. We all stopped and listened. It was the first time that he had played a keyboard and from that day on his need to play grew in him, grew in him so that eventually she saw fit to give him the expensive keyboard.

Michelle put a stop to his drinking during this time; if it hadn't been for that good Jewish girl, he wouldn't have written his final examinations.

38

Michelle loved D'nice. She loved the darkie brother. It went on and on, despite the fact that they both knew that the relationship was a cul-de-sac from the beginning – she was from a very powerful family and the music was just a way of killing time between now and when she found Mr Right, got married and had children.

Michelle was a celebrity in her own right. For those of you that have satellite television, she used to have a show on the Jewish channel as a teenager. Beautiful, thin, thin and tall as the world's models.

Not many people knew that D'nice was having it with her. They probably would have suspected something, but they were always told that D'nice was her music producer.

She is featured on the shelved kwaito CD by Cäres and, believe me, she was burning the pipe. She did justice to that song, which, at the time, I didn't believe she could.

I liked Michelle, liked her fearless character, liked the fact that she could just come to Hillbrow at night, park her car in Van der Merwe and walk herself to 207.

Well, we enjoyed her company and it was the first time I ever saw the underwear of a white girl.

D'nice was picked up by this big company before he even graduated. They gave him a very good job. He worked there for two months then handed in his resignation. When they asked why, he just said he wanted to quit, so they increased his pay by hundred per cent and put in a car. He worked for another month then resigned with immediate effect and told them no negotiations. They negotiated anyway, but his mind was made up.

There was music in his head and he wanted to get the music out.

Molamo

The writer, the director, the actor, the poet, the comedian, the producer, was once a tipper truck driver for a construction company. That
was, as he said, a great job. Just driving up and down. He drove that
ten-cubic-metre truck like Gugu coming out of that corner, whatever
they call it, at Khayalami racetrack with Sarel full in his mirrors (and
that's the right way to spell Khayalami). He pushed the truck so hard
that the manager didn't know whether to let him go or keep him.

The only problem was that after he'd had his last meal of the day,
after poking his pokiness, he'd start to feel uneasy and then he'd have
to fight to sleep. He thought that maybe the other drivers were jealous
of him and that maybe they wanted to kill him.

You know that thinking? It's another sad black story on its own. So
he went to the floor-shift people to check out what was wrong with
him.

You see, we are very funny people. A black man can kill you for living
your life, for trying to improve and better your life, and still come to
your funeral acting very hurt. Believe it happens. Believe me, I know.

Once I had a dear friend. He was very intelligent, matriculated with
six As, and won a scholarship. But, when he woke up a few days after
the celebrations and joy, he was not the same friend. His mind just
wasn't his. His mind had deserted him. The floor-shift saw this and told
me what their bones said. The prophets gave it their shot as well, and
told the very same story. But they couldn't retrieve his mind. His grandmother cried, but her grandchild's mind was gone and, eventually, he

died. Modern medicine could do nothing. Molamo consulted the floor-shift and they told him that he liked the job with his mind, but his heart didn't want him to drive trucks up and down. So he asked them, "What work does my heart want me to do?"

But the floor-shift didn't have an answer for that question.

"You can continue driving trucks, but that will result in something very bad happening to you," they told him, so he came back to dream city to have it out with the city. To dream it out.

He was a man who talked and talked. If you gave him a beer he'd talk forever. He'd tell you the story about his uncle who came to the dream city back in the days and got himself a city girlfriend.

When his uncle was making love to the girlfriend she started moving and shaking. He stopped and looked at her. She stopped, and so he continued, but the girlfriend shook on. Then he stopped and said, "I'm doing. You are doing. You're disturbing me. Stop that."

He continued pleasuring her, but she started doing it again. Then he got angry and stopped.

"What are you doing? I'm doing here. You want to do?"

He took a Seven Star out of his pocket and showed it to her. Then he continued, promising her, "If you do that again, I'll stab your butt."

Molamo had so many of them, those stories, and he told them so well that even if he was retelling one of them, one that you had heard twenty times before, you'd die laughing. There was one that I used to love and I could have listened to it a thousand times over. I would always push him to tell that story.

He had relatives in the township and like all township houses there was a back room, a boys' room. As the name suggests, it's where the boys live and are allowed to do whatever boys do. When you visited them, these boys would tell you that, as a boy, if you wanted to stay

41

with them in their boys' room, you'd have to poke one of the female species within seven days. If you didn't get lucky, you'd be back sleeping in the main house, and if you didn't believe that you could poke a female in seven days, you might just as well start sleeping in the main house right away. That was the right of citizenship to the boys' room.

Then, one day, one of their uncles from the rural areas visited. They didn't know how to tell him about the boys' room citizenship right. When they were about to sleep with heavy hearts, unable to do anything about the fact that he was going to sleep in the boys' room without the right to be there, he says, "I hear that there is a rule here that in seven days I must have slept with a woman in here or I have to sleep in the main house, is that true?"

"Yes."

"Then why didn't you tell me?"

"Ah! Well, now you know."

So on the eighth day, after supper, when the uncle was still having a late family chat, the boys disappeared with the key to the boys' room and the spare keys disappeared as well. True to the rule he had to sleep in the main house.

Talking about women; they gave Molamo a reason to live, or they once did. He had four children with four different mothers. The pictures that you saw on the wall of 207: they're his mirror images. They made him so sad sometimes that he'd suddenly take them off the wall. This always happened when he was lost to the war against the Isando god's disciples.

"I'm here living with the five of you in this one-room flat and what do I think they have eaten? What are they wearing? Do you think they are happy?"

What was I to say? He looked at me as if he expected me to come up with a comforting something, but no, I just gave him back the very same injured look that he had on. Then tears followed and I thanked myself for not having any children.

"It's not that I don't love my children. I love them as much as I love their mothers, but you know . . ."

He paused, looking at me, trying to fight the tears.

"You'll never understand."

Then, as soon as he was sober, they'd be back on the wall.

"I have them in my heart. I'm living for them and for them only."

He was lying to himself, not me, drowning even deeper in the problems of being a grown-up.

Tebogo was his lawyer woman, the sister with the money, the car and the townhouse. One day, their little boy didn't want to go to school – guess the boy got fed up with school for some reason. She took him to her boyfriend's place, the one who had a fleet of cars and a degree, then she brought him to 207 to see his father, who had neither a car nor a degree.

"Do you want to stay in a rented, single room with your five friends, like your father? Don't you want to drive very nice cars, have your very own house and enjoy your own money like Uncle Khutso?"

Note the "uncle". Khutso was his mother's boyfriend and a wannabe stepfather. He was trying with everything he had to get Tebogo to marry him. Molamo knew about the brother, knew that he was Tebogo's boyfriend, or keep-company as Molamo always called him. He wasn't threatened by him in any way.

Khutso was what the masses call the black elite. Young, black, under thirty and successful in financial terms. He had the world and all. This black elite in particular had two townhouses, a four-by-four and a couple of sports cars.

He'd pushed for four years at university without friends, without even a girlfriend. Taken refuge in books and in that way ensured his survival of UCT. He wasn't conscious of the damage done by those lonely-wishful four years; for him everything was possible because now there was money. He didn't have friends then, but now that he had money there were a million friends.

Khutso was expensive, a fashion parade, but all the pain and pressure that he'd felt when he was still poor was encoded somewhere in his heart. He always looked like he was trying to run away from it, looked like he was the richest man in the world.

"What is the difference between your father and Uncle Khutso?" his mother asked the other Molamo.

The other Molamo got the point and he never missed school again. The son didn't want to be like the father.

Molamo had saved some cash while driving that heavy-duty truck and, with that money, he entered himself in that great institution of tertiary education for the second time. Paid half the tuition fees up-front. This marked the start of his personal venture in dream city.

He always called himself the "thank you-man" because that was how he paid for things.

"My ladder to the top, every step that I have passed, has a face, that I have thanked, and those faces are holding me, this ladder, together."

You would be walking with him down Claim, going into the CBD, and he'd just stop to talk to this man or that woman from his past that he had thanked for something.

"Excuse the cliché, but no man is an island," he would tell you afterwards. "No one is a self-made something. People can help you with a very small something, and that can help you to be a very big something. I'm still dreaming a dream because of these people and the very

44

many things that they have done for me, and all they have had from me is a 'thank you'. If it wasn't for them, well, I don't know."

All the money he had saved dried up with the start of his second year. But he 'thank you'ed and 'thank you'ed until the great institution barred him from entering the examination room.

After all his hard work he became a dropout.

At the same time, Tebogo was writing her exams with a fifteen-month-old baby boy.

He'd tell you: "I packed my bags, bid farewell to this great city, but you need cash to get out of the city."

And with that he would make me remember that first day I came to the city.

We had just passed Witbank, we were running on the N12 in an aging Japanese-made taxi. Without any music and with fifteen passengers it was tense and kind of hostile. Nobody was talking. Maybe everybody was thinking about this great city, planning how they were going to do whatever it is that they were going to do there, do it better and in a quarter of the time. I smiled. Miriam Makeba's "Gauteng" was playing soft and sweet in my ears. Then I took a vow: When I come out of Gauteng I will be driving my own car. Well, I was still a teenager then.

Molamo was studying film and broadcasting at that great institution.

"I'm thankful that I didn't have the money to leave then because I would have gone. But I learned to survive in this great city. I'm still here, satan. I'm the 'thank you-man'. Let me tell you a secret: When you are with people, don't act powerful, be humble and weak; your body language should ask for protection, and you'll see much of the good in people," he said, sober as a lion.

He was from a farm. He went to primary school under the care of his

45

grandmother, which meant neglect. They had a saying on the farm: There is a crocodile in the water (meaning that you fear it, so you can't wash). Until he went to high school there was a crocodile in the water. He went through primary school without even a toothbrush. But that was not this Molamo. These days he was a fashion parade and had to wash each and every morning, then have a late-night bath with a book in his hand. He was the most expensive of the 207s; everything that he put on was heavily priced.

With eyes that he would claim could see people's souls and a permanent smile that made him look like he knew all things on, under and above God's green earth, this was Molamo.

Modishi

Solomon said that he had seen all things in God's green earth but he had never seen one honest woman in them all and had seen only one honest man in a thousand. In this thousand, Modishi was one such honest man.

How honest?

You wouldn't keep your secrets with him, he would tell. He'd start by saying, "Do you want to know a secret . . .?"

Not that he was stupid, he was just being honest.

The Zulu-boy nicknamed him John the Baptist, as he felt uncomfortable doing anything that was against his conscience, and if he did something to someone, three days wouldn't go past before he confronted the victim of the act and asked for forgiveness – relieving his heart. He once relieved his heart to Molamo: "Molamo, I'm sorry."

"For what?"

"I was thinking and wishing bad about you."

"So you are apologising, is that it?"

"Yes."

"The Baptist, you tell me what you were thinking first, then maybe I can forgive your overholy holiness."

"I was wishing that you die of Aids."

"Well, thank you! Where would I get it from?"

"From one of your beautiful girls. I know, it's not a good thing to think about someone."

"If I get it from a beautiful whore I'll forgive you and I will tell the fucking God to forgive you too and get Him to let you into heaven with a full pardon."

"Forgive me, please. I know you have nothing but good wishes for me."

Molamo looked at him, thinking that maybe this was the first time that he had ever hoped that something bad would happen to someone, and said, "The Baptist, that is not a sin. I think impure thoughts about people and wish that bad things will happen to them all the time, but you never hear me apologising to anyone. I have even had bad thoughts about you, but I have forgotten about them now. We all have people that influence those kinds of thoughts and you can't go looking for forgiveness every time, Modishi."

Sometimes I wish he hadn't come to live with us. He was one of the people that your heart, my heart, just disapproved of from the very moment I saw him. The bad part was that he never did anything bad to me. My blood just hated his blood and, as the years went by, I never really liked him much. This was a kind of relationship of disapprovals; my blood rejected his and maybe his rejected mine, but he never showed it. I didn't hate the man, I just didn't approve of him. I don't hate people.

Modishi wasn't interesting to me. He didn't even have an identity document at the age of twenty-two. He had only his balls and a matric certificate good enough to unlock the doors that bar the stupid from Wits and he wanted to . . . but that's a very long, sad black story. He discovered he could do music: a very quick-sure way to financial independence.

Wrong.

He lied to himself; there are no quick bucks there.

You need a quick buck?

Found a registered company and grow dagga, claiming you do it for cultural reasons. It's that simple.

Modishi wasn't exactly poor like you and me. He inherited hectares of land that had been laid waste since his father bowed out of this world. He would tell you, "It's been thirty years since that land was ploughed."

He would pause and the tears that couldn't be contained any more let themselves out.

"Even the chickens are no more."

We were sitting in front of the door to 207. Our legs were across the path so that people stopped and we had to pull up our drowning feet so that they could pass. These night people, some even cursed us, but that's the city, it has perpetual diarrhoea; don't let it get to you. The time: something to three. I can't remember what the occasion was, but whatever it was we really had had a good time.

Where was I?

Oh!

"Even the chickens are no more." That was how he ended the enlightening information about his past. At his farm there had been cows, sheep, goats, mules, donkeys, pigs and a black horse with a white blaze that was exactly the shape of the African continent, so they'd called it Africa.

There were two tractors of Swedish make, one Ford and one Massey Ferguson that was opened up.

They were all gone. His father's sister's husband knew where – he had his own herds now. Modishi's father didn't care about the farm and farming. He, like his child, had in him the need for the city, the love of the buzzing streets with neon lights.

Modishi always said that if he could make enough, he would move back to that land and give it life once more and stop suffering here in the lighted streets. Then I would ask him, "How much is enough, Modishi?" knowing that even if he made a million he'd never go back.

If he had been serious about it he could have gone long before he came to 207 and started farming the land with the money he had received from the sale of his house, or even have applied for a bank loan and grown from there. He was lying to himself, but that's dream city for you. It needs you and your Chinese thinking to keep you in it. It will city-ise you, hold you, lovingly caress you and orgasmify you and, by the time you wake up, it's too late: you're old, working as a barman, with four children from four different mothers and a maintenance order around your neck.

Talent is talent, everyone has it; you just have to want to do it and then you'll do it. He wanted to do music in this dreamer's city and he did it, first in Cäres, the failed group, with Matome, the Zulu-boy and D'nice.

I once believed that they were going somewhere, they even made it into the Sunday paper; to me it's another sad black story.

Modishi was an only child. His father was a man of high intelligence; a happy, lazy man who liked his jazz and a couple of bottles of beer for the rest of the day and couldn't wish for more than that. His mother was a coloured woman and she didn't do much more than sit around with her husband and a few friends, killing the day. They had a four-room house in Mapetla, Soweto. They were working piece jobs here and there, but his big business was supplying dagga, which he grew on the farm, to contacts that he had in the township. This was a very profitable business.

Tragedy struck while he was trying to outrun the police in his Valaza. He lost control, spilling the evidence in the street. And, with that, he guaranteed himself and his wife two tickets to the other life, the other life that we hope is far better than this one. Fortunately, Modishi was out playing with his cousins.

Twice fortunate for him, his relatives were not as greedy as some of us are. Although the farm was looted, he still had it when he turned eighteen. He even had the house in Mapetla. He sold the house to pay for his tuition fees and, feeling the peer pressures of dream city, he took most of the money and invested it in a four wheeler, but that got written off in less than a month.

He attended the great institution, paying for the whole of the tuition himself, studying sound engineering, only to discover at the time that they were preparing for the final examinations that the institution was not even registered. You know the story about these fly-by-night institutions of education that defraud the masses.

Modishi was big, so big that he couldn't even walk properly. Looking at him, you would have thought that he was an angry elephant that was going to trample over somebody. His complexion was dark and you wouldn't have guessed that his mother was coloured.

He could handle himself very well in all situations, and he excelled when he was on stage singing. He couldn't really dance, but you would have fallen in love with his voice and the way he changed it from tone to tone, and while D'nice, Matome and the Zulu-boy could dance far better than he could, he would complement them with his voice. He would drive the female species wild because he was the only one singing.

All this brings back those times when they were still pushing Cäres very hard and I was playing the part of the manager. I was always presented as the manager to everyone. Even though I had no knowledge of what a group manager is supposed to do. Then one of the female species would, sure enough, throw herself at me. And, of course, I would soften the landing for her. One would always want Modishi, who was never interested, and, if she was beautiful, I'd try to have her for myself. Get her number and tell myself that I was going to taste what the Venus had on offer. You only live once. I hope you know that too.

Modishi was a real one-woman man and that overly fortunate woman was Lerato. Honestly, I have never met one Lerato who is not beyond good-looking. The Leratos that I know, you can call them heavenly bodies, and this one in particular was one such heavenly body. If she had been a material she'd have had a sticker that said "handmade".

She had an abortion. These mothers of today who have rights!

Who cares? It is their right and their life.

This particular Lerato did it without telling a soul. Well, let me get you in on a scheme. You see, Modishi never used the condoms that our government gave us for free. He always used those very expensive ones – this was Lerato, she was worth it. She was a queen in his world.

The scheme: he went the first round condomed and for the second round, well, here's the scene as directed by Molamo:

MODISHI: Ah! I have run out of condoms.

LERATO: There are five boys living here and you tell me there are no condoms?

With that sweet voice she uttered these words from her wonderful mouth.

LERATO: Well then, go get some.

MODISHI: Let's just do it without this time.

There was a pause and the expected objection didn't come and silence meant consent. They did it without and they kept doing it without from that day on. Well, there were condoms in the closet and he had those expensive ones on him too, but we had put Modishi on a baby-making mission, put him under pressure telling him that he was twenty-three and didn't have a baby, while we all had more than one, except for me and Matome. So, he had decided that he wanted his own mirror image on this earth and he never asked Lerato.

Then, without telling him, Lerato got pregnant and had an abortion. I saw the changes and joked about it and then the Zulu-boy looked at her very carefully and said, smiling like he was the one responsible for her being like that, "Ja! She is pregnant."

Then she disappeared for about six weeks, only to reappear looking pale but not pregnant.

"Well! You were wrong," I told the Zulu-boy and he defended himself by saying that I was the one who had started it.

The second pregnancy. She couldn't live with herself and told Modishi that she was pregnant first. He came back to 207 and screamed it to us. We were all happy for him and a tiny bit jealous. He was Papa-coming and most of all he was very happy. Then, two weeks after celebrating, we were told that it was a false call, she was not pregnant after all.

I looked at her closely. I couldn't touch but I could tell that there was something wrong.

She lived with the two abortions until she couldn't keep it inside any more.

She called Modishi one day, just before school came out. He was in our haven, relaxing because he was going to work a night shift and so she came to 207 straight from school. She was looking worried, but that didn't worry him. She came with a pizza for him but she wouldn't allow him to eat it before she'd said what she had to say. They were sitting on the big bed.

"Modishi, I have to tell you something very serious first; I can't keep it inside any longer."

Then she started to sob and tears filled Modishi's eyes.

"Lerato, don't cry. Crying doesn't change a thing, whatever it is just forget it."

"Modishi, I have to tell you, I have to tell you because I will die if I don't. Modishi, I was pregnant that time I said I was pregnant."

Modishi looked at her, then looked down, but his vision faded and he closed his eyes.

"They said that I couldn't have the baby. Modishi, I know how much you wanted to have that baby, I could see it in your eyes that day I told you that I was pregnant and I knew that you wanted it all along."

He looked at the wall of fame and saw Molamo's painting of a baby, then he looked the other way and his eyes landed on a picture of Lebo. He didn't like what he saw in her and so he closed his eyes again, but the baby picture came to him, even with his eyes closed and so he opened them just as quickly as he'd closed them and looked down at his hands.

"Modishi, I wish I could say I'm sorry, and I am sorry, but there were reasons, valid reasons. I'm sorry, but I'm seventeen."

She was shaking, sweating, crying.

"And that was the second abortion. The first one I didn't tell anybody about."

She put her head between her thighs as if she couldn't bear to look at him any more.

"Modishi, say something because you make me feel like a whore."

He was crying too, the tears being pushed out. He was starting to get angry, but he still looked down at his hands as if not knowing what to do or to say.

54

They just sat there on the big bed. Then a question came into his mind: Lerato, when was this? But his tongue slipped and he said, "What's the use?"

"Modishi?"

She stood up, took her school bags and left our haven, slowly, like she was calculating how many small footsteps there were from the big bed to the front door, but she was just hoping he would say something.

"I love you."

And, with that, she gently closed the door and continued to walk very slowly, hoping that . . . but that didn't happen.

As she walked past the security checkpoint another pedestrian nearly ran her down, just in front of that old tree that had become a danger to the public, and my Venda vendor friend at the corner noticed her. She greeted him, as she had to get into a taxi a metre away from him, and it was him who told me that the grace was out of her.

John the Baptist – the Zulu-boy didn't give him that name for nothing. He stood up from the bed and put on some shoes. I always maintain that you can't understand a human being because a human being is not a finished book and I know that there is something that you don't know about yourself and the day you finally know about it you will not believe that you are that capable of that . . .

Modishi came back after eleven, he was supposed to be working in some downtown studio, engineering for a certain group. They kept calling and Lerato called too, but Modishi always left his phone when he knew he was going to be out late. We weren't worried about him, he knew his way around dream city.

This was the night that he had the conversation with the television leading to its sad and very crash-full end. His heart had moved from its rightful place and was choking him and the 207s were talking shit as usual.

He announced, "Lerato had an abortion."

It had got into his heart, but not into his soul yet, and he was definitely looking for some comfort, but you know how we are. Monna ke nku o llela teng, that's how we are supposed to be, how we were.

"These whores." D'nice's reaction. "They are all whores, there is nothing more you can do."

You just don't call a man's woman a whore. A woman, well, a girl, that he has told his heart to, that he wants, and wants her to be the only one in the whole world who deserves all that he is.

"Welcome to Johannesburg." That was Matome, he said it like pain was the only thing that was brewed in Johannesburg. The only thing that Johannesburg had in abundance.

"You are not the first and not the last. She's saved everyone a lot of misery and pain, not only the child but you as well," Molamo said, and Modishi's heart shifted a little to the right.

Whatever we said was just drowning him even deeper.

"At least you are still a free man," Molamo concluded, not considering that Modishi really wanted a child with Lerato.

The Zulu-boy looked at him, examining him pitifully, and offered him his hand, and Modishi, perhaps expecting some pity, offered his and they shook hands.

"You are the first person I know whose child has been aborted. I don't know what your ancestors are going to say about that," the Zulu-boy said, and we all cackled with laughter.

Then Modishi walked out to get some fresh air. When he came back, unable to eat, he had the conversation with the television and told us the whole story and still we had no comforting thoughts.

56

How do you comfort a man? It's not there in komeng, there is no lesson for comforting darkie brothers. Real men don't need comforting. Their hearts and souls comfort them, they never cry and if they do, no one sees their tears.

"Lerato had two abortions within the space of a year," Modishi repeated, trying hard to get us to see the seriousness of this act.

What do you say? How do you give comfort to a man's heart? If it had been me, I would have done her harm.

The Zulu-boy was the only one who tried. He looked him in the eye, and I know from experience that there was nothing but violence in his heart, but what he said made sense: "Modishi, she had the abortions but getting mad doesn't help. You should forgive her first and then decide if you still want her back, but stop being mad at us. Smile and eat your food, you are not the first and definitely not the last, Mr Baptist."

When my old man was buried and everyone was feeling sorry for me, trying to comfort me while I cried, my uncle came to me, took my hand and squeezed it very hard so that I felt physical pain.

"Who was in that casket?"

I looked at him and he squeezed harder.

"Dad."

"He is dead. Stop crying and be a man. Crying will not bring him back. You are on your own now. You're on your own."

So, from that day on, I never had a reason to cry or the need for comforting. I stopped crying and became a man. How do you expect me to give comfort to another man?

The story was that Lerato told her mother that she was pregnant as she didn't know what to do about it. Her mother told her godmother, who had even bigger reasons for her not to have a baby, and so the two mothers in her life made her do it.

Modishi loved Lerato like he gave birth to her; their love was that of a mother and child. I know that Modishi never had sex with another woman. Sometimes I envied him that kind of love – to love one woman no matter what she did. To respect her and fear her as well.

Two and a half weeks after the shocking news, they were dating again and doing it again in 207.

Talk about love is the answer.

She called a day after telling the truth and a hurt Modishi just looked at his phone, let it ring, and then, after it stopped, switched it off. She left a dozen messages. Not one was listened to.

Sometimes, we all take for granted the power that one's heart has over one. Within a week Modishi looked like he'd lost about twenty-five kilograms. He'd lost interest in all worldly things and spent most of his time hiding on the floor next to the balcony door, the other side of the big bed. You would come into 207 and do your thing, whatever it was, but if you never thought of going out onto the balcony you would think that you were alone.

"Time has come to search for another Lerato. Because, however you think of whores, the structure is the same and the character matters but, in the end, they all serve the same purpose," Molamo said victoriously to Modishi, remembering an argument that had nearly gotten out of hand when the Zulu-boy and Molamo were trying to make Modishi into what they were.

Modishi defended what he was, that which he believed in, saying, "In a woman, what matters is the woman's character. The structure of a woman is the structure of all women and serves the same purpose, you can replace a woman with a woman and still get the same things that you had with the first one, but you can't replace one woman's character with another's."

58

"The Baptist, it is time to search for another Lerato," Molamo continued, smiling in a way that said I hate to say this but I told you so long ago.

"It sounds like a cliché, doesn't it? Time to hit search engines, search for another Lerato; if it does, excuse it."

Matome looked at Modishi, felt sorry for the brother, and I thought: Is this what love can do? Then Matome said, "Baba, you can forgive the beautiful Lerato, can't you?"

But, even as he said it, Molamo continued provoking him. "Modishi, I don't know what to say if a man like you is crippled by what a little girl did. Yes, she looks twenty-three but she is still seventeen. Let's go out and I can give you someone, a real woman, one you can abuse as you want and they can abuse you back. One who can replace Lerato as a character and as a woman."

Modishi stood up and looked at him. "The character in Lerato is not worth losing because even if you live another lifetime, you'll never have one like her. All you have are whores, gold-diggers and bitches."

"Thank you, thank you very much but you missed something: my whores, gold-diggers and bitches served four times a purpose that she's aborted twice."

You couldn't argue with Molamo, Modishi knew that and so he looked him in the eye and did the thing which he knew would hurt him most.

"I forgive Lerato and I'm taking her back, she is my whore, gold-digger and bitch."

"Darkie mense, darkie mense, darkie mense."

"Forgive her. She is lucky to have you in her life but I don't think you are as lucky to have her."

"I forgive her."

"Darkie mense, darkie mense, darkie mense." Matome raised his voice, trying to dilute whatever was brewing between Modishi and Molamo.

Then Modishi went to the bathroom to take a bath after nearly two and a half weeks without washing.

* * *

Modishi called Lerato and they met in Cresta. In less than an hour's time, they were sitting on the green grass overlooking the parking lot, not knowing where to start. He started looking at the cars in the lot, thinking like a thief. Then he started to think about Klerksdorp, so long ago, when he was still a teen and out to conquer the world. He put on a smile as he thought of some of his high-school friends and his cousin Thabiso in particular. Thabiso, who had the heart and balls to risk it, a smile and a laugh to laugh out loud in the face of danger. Then he was thankful to lack a heart and balls big enough . . .

"Sometimes it helps to be a fool."

Lerato missed the point.

"Thabiso died because he knew too much and pretended to know it all."

"Who's Thabiso?"

"A funny cousin I had once; with him everything was possible. You would like him but unfortunately you'll never get to know him."

"What happened to him?"

"He was never a fool, nobody could fool him."

"Modishi, I'm sorry, I wasn't fooling you; I couldn't fool you because you are not a fool."

"Lerato, I'm sorry to take advantage of our love and do things because I want them. Sure, I wanted you to have the baby and that's why

I stopped using condoms. I'm sorry for putting you in that position. You can blame it on me because that wasn't your doing. Lerato, I am sorry and I want you to take me back, please." A few tears took over and she began to cry too. "Because, right now, I'm the one who is feeling like a whore."

She hugged him.

They signed their peace agreement with a kiss and a car nearby hooted in appreciation.

"We are going to call our first-born Thabiso," she said and he responded, "When we want to have him?"

"Yeah! When the time is right to."

With that, Lerato forgave Modishi. He asked for forgiveness for all his wrongdoings and Lerato forgave him and took him back. Modishi was the one upright and honest man that Solomon spoke of. I sometimes felt sorry for him, for what he stood for and believed in, because it wasn't something of this world. But, most of the time, I envied him. He was a three-and-a-half-year-old toddler in the body of a twenty-three-year-old man.

Zulu-boy

If there is anyone you know, always telling you that they have lived the ins and outs, days and nights of Hillbrow, they are lying. Most of them don't like it there; they hate the place. Everybody is on their way out of Hillbrow.

But there was one man, a Hillbrowean in true nature, who not only lived the good life of the place but felt its very painful existence as well. He breathed it and so it breathed him, it embraced him and he embraced it, felt its pain and made it feel his pain.

Zulu is the unofficial language of the street, it rules the streets, has power and command in it. All Zulu men are like the greatest king of the Zulu nation, Nkosi Shaka, who killed his own child, tore apart his very own genes.

What is my point?

All Zulu men are violent, always talking hard and commanding. No one was ever robbed by a Venda-speaking man. Every robbery is done by the Zulu or, let me say, done in Zulu.

He had been mugged a dozen times and he had mugged others a dozen times. Not that he went out with the intention of robbing someone. No. That someone just presented himself to be robbed.

There are things that you don't do when you are in dream city. He twice took phones from men. One was being driven in an expensive German car. He was talking on the phone with the window open. The Zulu-boy greeted him, took it and continued moving like nothing had happened.

The other one was taken on a hot day from a man who was sitting in the back of a taxi with the window open.

This was the Zulu-boy. He was not exactly an average Zulu because Zulu men are well-built men and he was average height and thin, he looked more Zim than Zulu and because of that the police always stopped him (that was why he always moved around with his ID book).

He had a very small head, with a scary scar on his jaw, inches away from his right ear, that looked like a show dolphin. His right ear had three piercings, where three diamonds were hung to neutralise the scar. He had another scar just above his chin and that made him, well, not pleasant to look at. He didn't like to smile much, and if he did, it would mean that he was comfortable with all the people around him, which was unusual. He got even harder if there was one of the female species with him that he was poking, or having the need to poke.

His voice was always strong, well projected and powerful; there was never a need for him to repeat what he had just said because you would have heard him the first time.

He was not expensive, he was a style man, and all his "expensive" material was always bought through the back door. He would stop at a street vendor's stall and look at something with interest. He would want to pay forty per cent and there would be no negotiating. If the vendor happened to be a lekwerekwere, he would want to pay under thirty-five per cent and the poor vendor would not even get a thank you.

Then he would take his time looking in the mirror, making whatever it was sit on him like he had a PhD in fashion. You would have liked him and thought that he was very expensive, and that was what everybody thought about him until they were walking in the street and saw the exact same garment.

When he first came to the city he stayed in Ponte, the building with the biggest electric billboard on the top. It was a very clean place then, but it has turned into another sad story on its own. He was a student at the technikon, studying sound engineering, but then he became a victim of that thing we call peer pressure, which is one thing that all students have in their student life.

Sometimes I think that the Zulu-boy just liked things, liked attention and liked to show off. He was arrested a couple of times for silly crimes. Crime was his way of putting up with the Ices of the institution – he came from a celebrated family and expected himself to be a trendsetter, but he failed at that. He failed at trying to keep up with his peers and so he became another peer pressure dropout.

After he left Ponte he lived on the outskirts of Braamfontein, on Hospital Street in Dudley Heights. He never spoke about what he was doing at this time, he was just like Matome sometimes, but the rumour was that he was living with a woman twice his age, a woman who had everything. He got her pregnant and they had a baby. You can think of the end yourself.

He stayed on Captain Street in Brenton Manor for a short time. Then he stayed in Marriston Hotel on Claim Street, pushing drugs. He got arrested and was in prison for nine months waiting for trial; then, somehow, the case was dismissed due to a lack of evidence. On his release he vowed not to do crime any more.

It was when he was staying at the Ambassador that he met Matome. The day after they met, he came to the studio to prove to Matome that he could engineer sound. Matome rejuvenated his dream, freed it from its dream-heaven, and he made it into Cäres and that's when the real dreaming started.

He loved the city and understood every soul in it. The only thing that he would have changed about it would have been to make everybody in it Zulu. If he had had the chance, he would have made everyone in Johannesburg a Zulu.

Though he didn't like makwerekwere, he hated the Pedis even more. He associated every individual with their tribe or the land that they were from. For him, the Zulus were the supreme race and after that everybody was subhuman, "lamaPedi".

Don't blame him, he inherited that from somewhere in our past. No matter what you were, if you were black, he liked to know what tribe you were from. To him, every man had the mentality of his tribe.

The Zulu-boy was different, he had seen that day we were all waiting for – the day when we would have the biggest party Hillbrow had ever seen. Until that day came he was just going to enjoy Hillbrow to the full.

The first time I came here, like so many of us I had heard stories about Hillbrow being the capital of sin.

"Stay away from the ways of the city, my child; you are there to get an education and not to get the ways of the city. Don't let the ways of the city into you," my grandmother told me when I was leaving home for the city.

But I came to understand the city ways, love them even, and Hillbrow isn't a capital of sin, it's just a residential area, where people are living and trying to make a living. After slaving, after school, after the formal part of our lives, we mingle and mend, use and abuse what we can use and abuse while hoping to never get used and abused ourselves. Those are the ways of the city.

The Zulu-boy found love somewhere in the middle of what the holy ones of this God's green earth call sin.

Courtesy of Matome and his no-strangers lifestyle, he got acquainted with the city's angels of the night. They too are people, the same as you and me, with hopeful dreams. I once hated them more than you do, but I came to see that they are human beings too, and so did the Zulu-boy. And then he fell deeply in love with one of them.

Noughts
and
Dreams

Welcome to Johannesburg

I have been to Cape Town. I have been to Durban, Bloemfontein, Nelspruit and Polokwane. I have been to Grahamstown. I have never been to Lagos and that goes for New York and London too. But the best part of it is that I don't want to live in any of them. I don't even want to visit any of them. I have Johannesburg and I can't ask for more.

Johannesburg. It's a city founded by some people.

Who cares that they founded it here? The British had their time here and it passed. The Afrikaners had their time; they enjoyed it, and then it too passed by. Now Johannesburg is under the control of the black man, his time is here and, by the looks of things, his time will never pass.

Johannesburg. This is the land where the weak, the poor, the rich and the powerful – powerful enough that they can rob you of your own life – mingle and mend, excuse the cliché.

I once ran into them, one late night. Put myself in a position to be robbed and like always the robbers rose to the occasion. I had lost my mind to the pleasures that the female species can offer to a man, and then I lost my direction. I didn't see that I was presenting myself as a potential victim, you never realise it until it is too late, and, by the time I realised, I was looking at a wall.

You never know in Johannesburg, but, I tell you, walk carefully and think fast; this is Johannesburg, you are either fast or dead.

Well, I am a man and so I tried to fight them: my second mistake.

There were three of them. They pinned me down. Zulu boys. They were speaking Zulu. So, with that went the cellphone, the expensive watch and R132. They even took the 77 cents. These poor-hungry-unemployed darkie brothers of the city. They even took my shoes before they left me bleeding.

Let me advise you: these people will kill you for your own property. So next time they want your . . . please, give it to them as fast as you can and save that life. However manly you are, they are expecting you to fight and they need to pay the rent. Please, don't die to pay their rent, because even though you are annoying we still need you breathing somewhere-somewhere in this rainbow nation.

By the time I got to 207, I had stopped bleeding. Matome looked at me, smiled knowingly and said, "Welcome to Johannesburg, baba."

I laughed.

And you're thinking: What's so funny?

Well, nobody had ever welcomed me to Johannesburg. He, Matome, had organised a flat party for me and I had been living with him for four years in this city and here he was, welcoming me like it was my first time. That was Matome, he didn't even want to know what had happened to me.

"Welcome to Johannesburg. This time you really felt it, your blood has been spilt and mixed with its soil. You and the city are in perfect connection with each other. Your blood runs in its veins as it runs in your blood," said Matome.

In the old days, the very good-gone-by-never-coming-back old days before even the word hospital was invented, the umbilical cord was cut, mixed with the mother's blood from the labour and then the elders would bury the mixture. The elders would be of the child's sex and they would, in the middle of the night, take the mixture and bury it in the middle of the cattle kraal to announce to the gods of the soil that there was a new arrival. In this way they would ask that the soil nurture him, give him plenty, guard him and never reject him. Not only would the soil know him, he would know the soil because they would be one.

"Welcome to Johannesburg."

Indeed, welcome to Johannesburg.

Long after I had recovered, and forgotten that I ever got robbed, I'm doing harm to boredom in the central library with a few books in a favourite corner by the big window that I have made my own. Behind me Jo'burgers are going up and down, up and down, serving the rand. We are all loyally serving money.

Then, as I read, I hear this voice.

"Welcome."

I listen carefully, looking around, wondering who it was. I'm alone, there's no one sharing my corner with me today, and the people outside can't even see me.

"Welcome."

Then I think that maybe I'm dreaming. I shake my head, and look down at the book that I'm carefully reading.

"Here you'll have a home."

I pinch myself and stand up. True, I'm not dreaming, I'm really in the library. Then a man comes around looking for his favourite book, but the voice continues.

"Don't let anything scare you, you are home now. Welcome."

I sit down again, wiping away the sweat, but I'm willing to listen to the voice because I have a voice somewhere too – a voice that I can engage in a very intellectual conversation and share a laugh with. But this isn't the voice inside me.

God, when He comes, comes as a voice as well. But this is not God.

"Who was that?" I asked the voice inside me.

Johannesburg. You are now officially welcomed in Johannesburg.

Shutdown days

Sometimes I think it's very funny. Six men sharing a single-room flat and failing to pay the rent on time.

"We are freelancers," I try to justify our situation to myself. "We do no ordinary work. Sometimes money doesn't come to our pockets and then dreaming in this city becomes very hard, and there's nobody you can ask to loan you some cash that you'll return when the days are good."

What's that? Call my father and ask him for some cash?

No, that is not a very good idea.

"Son," he would say to me.

"Dad."

"I think that you have an ID, right?"

"Yes."

"And some years ago you passed your matric, is that right too?"

"Yes."

"And you have a driver's license. And you also have a passport, don't you?"

"Yes, I have but –"

"Don't 'but' me, I'm still talking here."

Pause.

"Son, you have your girlfriends. How many are they? Remind me?"

Pause.

"I only know four, there is that one from . . . I don't think that you are still interested in that one with a big behind and I thought that she would make a good wife, she really did want you. And maybe there are still some that I don't know about? I think there are."

I was amazed that he knew all my girlfriends.

"What does all this that you have accomplished make of you, my son?"

Pause.

"Now you can talk. It is your time to talk."

He looked at me right in the eye and I couldn't bear to return that look.

"Look at me. Talk to me, man to man. What does all this that you have achieved by yourself make you, my son? All these things that you have, son. They make me very proud of you. That you have a passport means that you can go to lands far away and your father has never been far. I never had a passport. Have never been to any other country. But you have a passport, son. You have been to Lesotho."

He wipes away what I think is a joyful tear.

"You just said, 'Dad, I'm going to Lesotho.' Didn't I ask you with what? But you went there and you came back.

"All these things make you a man and that is why I want you to look at me in the eye and talk to me, because you are now a man. The sole fact that you have not a girlfriend but girlfriends makes you a complete man and that makes me very proud of you because, man, you went out and got yourself girls without soliciting anybody's help. Isn't that so? Is that not so?"

"Yes, it is."

"So why can't you continue being on track? You are taking yourself off the track. Be a man, not an image of one. A man stands on his own two feet and fights his own wars. And now you want to disappoint me. You are not a child any more and I did what I could for you. If I failed you, well, you have you. You now have to make right the failures that I have made in your life, make them right because I can't, I did all that I can and now it's all on you."

That was my old man. And that was the last time I ever asked for anything from him.

I could get a job at the supermarket, but the problem would be that I would devote myself to the supermarket and like Molamo, when he was driving, I would find myself fighting to sleep.

Well, I like this dreaming business anyway.

* * *

It's the seventh.

Every month on the seventh, a beautiful Xhosa woman, a slave of the landlord, wakes us up, with her over-sweet voice to remind us that we have not paid this city thing called rent, which was supposed to be paid by the third.

I look at her make-upped face. I don't know what it's supposed to do, this make-up: enhance her beauty or sedate it? Like every soul in this Johannesburg she has her very own sad fairy tale to tell.

She was still young, her beauty indefinable. And, let me tell you, she loved it, revelled in it. Believe me, beauty has some element of power.

I asked her once, "Do you know Ice?"

"Justice!" that angel voice responded in a surprised tone. "Where is he?"

Well, she knew Ice. Like the man said, you just ask anybody and they'll tell you. I told her that he was Matome's friend, knowing full well that even if she saw the man's remains she wouldn't recognise him.

She has four children, the first-born is eleven and the youngest is less than two. The make-up hides the scars and the troubles that her own beauty has caused her. Most of her dreams are in dream-heaven, taking indefinite refuge.

After she leaves, the electricity is always switched off. She switches it off somewhere. We still have some hot water though, but take care that Matome doesn't use it all. I wash after him, brush my teeth, comb my hair and then I'm out.

Now I face another problem. These slaves of the landlord are going to remind me, us, every time we walk through this castle's gates that we haven't paid them their rent. They are going to remind me right now and they are going to remind me of the very same thing when I come back. What can I say? How can I explain that six men don't have anything with which to pay for their very own castle?

These slaves, they're not that bad; they are black and they understand. It is just that they have a master. These darkie brothers are just doing their job and we are making their job very hard for them.

Considering that they let the six of us share 207 with perpetual visits from the female species, they seldom complain. Even the other tenants don't complain, and they should, we're paying the same amount for electricity and we should be paying three times the amount.

The fact is that we never really see the good side of people; we only notice the bad things.

Shutdown days do end. They only last for two days. After two days of darkness and nagging reminders, which become like a number one hit on the kwaito charts, comes the lockout, lasting till we pay.

They like to do it very early in the morning. The sedated beauty will be the only one talking. She's the manager here, leading the house security guards, four of them, just before they are about to change shifts.

It's a sad feeling to have people locking you out of your haven. What does it really say about you? Although we are laughing on the outside, inside it's a very different story.

*   *   *

It's six o'clock exactly.

The landlord's slaves come, mustering their courage – no smiles, no talking.

Sometimes Matome will pull a joke on them, keeping the money till they come to lock us out and then he'll pay them at the door, but not today.

Modishi just takes his bag, that he packed days before, and walks out without saying anything.

D'nice is speaking his mind, trying to convince them not to lock us out, but only really succeeding in annoying them further: "People, we are living here. I mean. People, this is not good."

He looks at the make-upped one. She is without make-up now and the reasons are very plain why she had to have it on in the first place.

"We are going to pay you eventually. We know we have to pay rent, it is just that we don't have it right now. What's locking us out going to do? If we don't have the money, we don't. It is not like we have it and we don't want to pay. And we can't have the money just because you lock us out. We know we have to pay you. We are renting this place."

However hard he tries to make them see the point, they are working on rules, regulations and procedures. They have already been more than considerate; they should have locked us out two days ago.

The Zulu-boy looks at them with angry eyes and says loudly, "Xhosa."

She doesn't respond to that, as it seems that if she were to respond he would do her harm. Then he looks at the security guards and says, "Other people don't deserve to be Zulu, they make my nation seem only good for being a nation of security guards. Fuck!"

True enough: Zulu men make exceptional security guards.

She tries to cut in, not sure of herself, feeling the anger that wasn't their fault but was directed at them, "We are not here to fight."

"Xhosa, who is fighting with you?"

But the landlord's slaves are here to unhaven our haven. We have been waiting for them for five days. We're making their work hard as it is. I just brush my teeth, and comb my hair. Take a bag with the few things that I need to survive wherever I'm going to lay my head, which will be at Wada's place.

Matome's already there. He didn't want to be in this scene, the scene where they are locking us out – locking us out, not because we couldn't afford to pay, but because we have given the money away, used it for other, joyful things.

We always give all our money to that great god of Isando without thinking of this day that we know will come. We always pay late or get locked out, but we never pay on time.

They remind me, as I am leaving, that we have ten days to pay or other people will move in and then, when we need our things back, we'll have to pay twice the amount to get them.

Then Matome is opening the door to Wada's place, and saying, "They finally closed you out, baba, welcome."

Wada's home

Wada is Matome's partner in everything. He is Matome's clone. Not that he doesn't have a mind of his own. No. The man has a matric certificate that could guarantee entry to every university – even the ones in heaven.

Then why is he waiting here for a death certificate?

Allow me not to say, please, that he is another sad story and I hope you understand now.

Wada is a township Zulu boy and speaks township Zulu, not that rich Zulu from the Valley of a Thousand Hills like Zulu-boy. He too is a conman: the singer cum businessman cum producer cum manager cum something-and-everything cum DJ Baby Wada Da.

Wada's homes were always in the city centre. When I first knew him he was staying at Pan Africa House, on the corner of Troye and Jeppe Streets, then he moved to Lekton House in Wanderers Street, on the corner of Bree Street, and from there to Johannesburg Park Station.

That's where we are now: Johannesburg Park Station.

"They finally closed you out, welcome," Matome says, smiling because he knows how I knock at the door.

Welcome. Indeed, welcome to Wada's home. It's a big room, as you can see, a hall, to be honest.

The blankets on the floor?

That is where he sleeps. Notice the four computers and, if you look carefully, there are five printers all stuck because of a lack of ink. Don't mind the clothes on the chairs, they were washing them yesterday.

Find a chair and sit.

If you are lucky enough you'll get to see Wada ironing his clothes on Wada's ironing board, which is the floor.

The dirty water in the bath?

They were washing; these boys share a bath here, Matome and Wada.

"Hey! It's a secret, don't tell anybody."

There's nothing that has to do with hygiene here, everything is for survival. Matome and Wada, if it ever came to it, they'd share a condom.

Welcome to Wada's home.

You want some coffee while they are still preparing for this day?

No?

Thank you, you just saved a cup for somebody else. You need anything?

No?

Thank you again, and don't say to people that we're not hospitable, because you thanked us for our hospitality and never felt it. You can now close your eyes, please.

Hocus-pocus.

Open your eyes. It's seven o'clock. Elliot and Omega, the second and third of Matome's trusted slaves, are here – Matome's most trusted employees. Omega asks us to stand up and put our hands together, as he opens the day's business with a prayer, "Dear God . . . Amen."

You are in Matome's office now and he is open for business.

Matome always maintained that he could, if it came to it, go to Lagos for free. Just get on the runway and hike a plane. One is bound to stop.

We just died laughing. But, true enough, he always tries to do things

80

at a next-to-nothing price, but then we never have money enough to do anything anyway. But not having enough doesn't mean that you don't do.

The underground musicians were all, as always, putting too much hope in Matome, hoping that he would make them all household names. I've seen the hope in their faces as they start their association with Matome and their satisfaction when he delivers their CDs, with their names and pictures on the covers – all at their expense. Their joy when their song gets played on one of the big radio stations, and they have an interview or an article in the paper, courtesy of Matome and his no-strangers lifestyle. He has friends in all the places he wants them.

They always call Matome with satisfaction in their voices and, the day they come to the office, they won't mind paying some more, paying for something – nothing that they don't understand. Matome is that good.

"Beautiful, I don't have a gun, don't own one and don't intend on ever having one. I'm not a killer. I consider myself a businessman and you say I'm a hustler. I don't put a gun against people's heads, I don't trick anybody. They give me their money willingly."

This was how he justified himself when one of those intellects that I was dating felt that he was taking people for a ride.

One day he smiled, amazed, not really believing that he was doing what he was doing: the impossible.

"Someday they are going to kick me. Worse, they are going to shoot me, or I'm going to be more than rich. Those are the only two options in my life. There are only two roads in my life and I am going to travel one and I'll be reaping what I have sown."

* * *

Tick-tick-tick the time is going. Now I have to get a job. Go down the stairs with a broadcasting directory and make a public phone my own.

"Hi, hello! I'm a dropout student of film due to some financial difficulties and . . ."

I go on begging, but they always do the same things. The secretary will pass me to somebody who, if he or she listens, will say that I should fax them my CV and he or she will try by all means to get back to me, which they never do. Sometimes they're asking for my CV for the fifth time.

Matome always says, "I don't want a job, don't want to work for Sony or EMI. Brains Records is my life, I'm building it from nothing with nothing. There is no child who was born walking; all things have to grow from one point to another."

Then he'll turn on me and say, "You want a job? Stop wanting it and do the job. Go out there and raise the money needed to make a feature film and make it. Talk to people, one of them is bound to give you an ear. Then, after that, the money will be running after you."

That is the hard part. I have been trying for seven years. I have more than ten film scripts back there at 207, all in need of some cash injection so that they can die a script life and live a reel life.

At first, I thought I was let down because I was black, but then I found that black brothers didn't want to listen either. But that kind of talk, Matome's kind of talk, can give you hope and start you off all over again.

But, in the end, it doesn't matter how much hope you have. You're still going to be confronted with that one question: "I like your script. It's good, very good, but why do you think that your script is going to make money as a film?"

Pause.

"Do you honestly believe it will make money?"

Pause.

"Schuster is selling because he's got a big reputation and you have nothing."

But it is my work and I believe in it.

* * *

Sitting in Matome's office playing games, playing a secretary, will get to you, but the library is available at no cost at all and it will never get to you. You can just walk in and consume as much information as you can without even saying hello to anyone. I pull out Richard Rive's *Buckingham Palace, District Six* and live District Six, Cape Town, nineteen-something, and by the time I pull myself out of District Six they want to close the library.

I take out six books for the night.

Wada's home is not a very good place to be, but then we are going to live there for a couple of days, maybe less or more, you just never know.

* * *

When I get back to Matome's office I find that they are still doing business. I've got a rumbling tummy, the sea is rough, and, so as not to listen to it, I dip my head between the lines and become *Adrift on the Nile.*

Hocus-pocus.

It's eight now and slowly we, there is an evolution here, lose the formality. This is no longer Matome's office. Talk shit if you want. Once again welcome to Wada's, you are in Wada's home now. The hotplates are out and the clothes have just been washed and are hanging on the chairs.

Tonight Molifi is here with us and the night is still very young. They'll talk about the whole of this life and the future as well. I've had some coffee and dry bread but I'm not full. Then I think of Dudley Heights. I can solve my stomach stresses and other things there.

I pretend to take a walk, but in fact I am intending to visit Hospital Street and de-stress: "I'm taking a walk, Matome. Are you coming with me?" I lie.

I'm not really inviting him to come with me – I know that even if I wanted him to come with me he wouldn't come.

"Why, baba? Where are we going?"

"Are you coming?"

"Where?"

Then I walk out of Wada's home.

* * *

Pass the security checkpoint. Into a lift, to the fourteenth floor, then into 1410 and the first thing she says is: "What's your problem?"

Maybe she's reading the troubles painted on this face.

"Nothing but the city and its stress."

With that I invite no more questions, because there's nothing she can do to help and so she doesn't have to know.

I de-stress and leave, because no girlfriend deserves to see my sleeping face and try to figure out what is on my mind, wonder what my nightmares, sweet or sad, are all about and then have the nerve to ask the next morning.

I de-stress and leave her to herself. I am feeling livelier.

* * *

When I get back to Wada's they are still talking poverty.

I call my fiancée and detect something in her tone that says that she doesn't want to talk to me. I can always detect it and it usually comes out when she is with a male friend. So I cut the connection without even saying goodbye. She won't call back unless there was no one there, then she'll call back pretending to be angry, saying, "Why is it that you cut the phone in my ears?"

My fiancée is another person in my life whom I can't really figure out. I can't say it's love, love always wears out. I can't say it's trust either, trust has jealousy in it. But I can say it's an equilibrium between two minds.

Once, I bought a teddy bear and gave it to her, and she looked at it and said, in that angel voice of hers, "Do you know that everything has a meaning and implication?"

"Yeah," I said with a smile, trying to be charming.

"And what is the meaning of this?"

Pause.

"What does you giving me a teddy bear mean?"

"It means I love you."

"And what does it imply?"

"That I love you."

"No," she said with an angry tone in her voice.

"What did I do wrong now?"

"If you want me to have your baby, I'm not ready to have a baby. The time is not right for me to have a baby yet."

"I don't want you to have a baby."

"The teddy bear implies that you are ready to have a baby. That's why you're giving it to me and, by accepting it, it means I want to have a baby too. That is the message I'm getting here about the teddy bear."

She took it that I was giving her a teddy bear because I wanted to say that I wanted to have a baby. Very, very practical, my fiancée.

I lie flat on the floor and go *Adrift on the Nile*, trying hard not to think about how many days this lockout is going to last.

By half-twelve I've finished drifting on the Nile. I try to be a sympathetic undertaker, but the eyes have had enough, so I join the poverty talk and talk poverty.

Then the time to sleep comes, the early-morning hours – after one but before three o'clock. There are only two blankets here, no pillows and no bed, not even a sponge, and then there are four of us. I'm lucky tonight: I'm sleeping in the middle with Matome, Molifi and Wada on the sides. They'll be the ones to fight for the blanket. But, actually, there is never any tugging – we sleep like logs, we don't even bend or turn.

At half-past five a phone alarm begins to ring, ring and ring. Wada gets up and silences it and then we doze again until half-past six, when Matome wakes up roaring, "People, it's time to wake up, I'm waking up. Time to wake up," or Wada just pulls off the blanket and is on his feet like he is an Umkhonto we Sizwe guerrilla waking up to the sound effects of R1s.

Then they are rushing, everything is in a rush – this place has to be Matome's office by half-past seven. We were supposed to wake up at half-five, now everything is in a rush-rush.

Wada is shouting and generally being irritating, like he's someone's wife readying the kids to go to school, but I just close my ears and eyes and relax; maybe he likes doing that but it doesn't bother me, I'm used to it.

I take the blanket and nap. If you can call it that. I bend and twist for the few minutes that I can manage. I never smell and I always, if it comes to it, take advantage of this fact. I only need to brush my teeth and comb my hair and then I'm ready for a new day.

Hocus-pocus.

You are in Matome's office and he, we, Brains Records is open for business.

Weekending

"Black people, we are not happy people," Molamo observes.

"But are you happy, Molamo?" Matome asks.

"I am not happy, Matome. I pretend to be a happy individual, but look at me, look at me carefully. Let me lay my life out for you: I have fathered four children, but I am not a father; I use and abuse every female and leave them crying. How long has Tebogo mothered and wifed me? But I have always used her. Worse, I even call her a whore and she is the mother of my first-born child."

He is talking very slowly, as if these things need time to sink in, then he pauses and looks at Matome.

"Do you then think that I am happy?"

And, as he asks that question, he's suddenly back to being the Molamo that we are all used to.

"What we are deep inside reflects in us as a nation, as Africans. You all, like me, like to believe that you are all happy. What I have seen is that we have a personal, national hate. We don't like ourselves. In each and every one of us there is no love but hate and anger."

He pauses, while we all look at him, waiting for him to continue explaining.

"Molamo, is there hate and anger in you?"

"Yes."

"Molamo, you are happy, you have anger, hate and love as an individual and you will reflect that in the community and the community will reflect that in the nation. You and all of us are like that, which then makes us a happy and loving nation that in some degree has anger and hate."

"Can you repeat what you just said, satan?" the Zulu-boy breaks his silence. "Explain yourself further, please."

"People universally have all emotions in them: love, hate, anger, fear, happiness. And all that will always reflect in us as a nation," Matome explains, while Molamo looks at him, picking his nose.

"I love myself," argues Matome, "so listen to me very carefully."

We all look at him, Molamo and the Zulu-boy waiting for him to cross that invisible line. Should he cross it, they will brutalise him.

He knows well that he is about to cross a line.

"I love myself and I'm proud of myself, proud of my blackness."

He pauses, a long pause with some knowing smiles.

Molamo interrupts the silence: "A hateful love, a blind self-pride and artificial black proud-ness: that is what I am looking at in all my black brothers and sisters; exactly what I am looking at in you, Matome, in all of us. Look deep in your hearts, sisters and brothers, we are not happy people."

We're all looking at him, trying to get to the state of revelation that he's in.

"Why do you say that, Mr Know-it-all?" a sweet voice asks. It belongs to Lerato and it still had its innocence intact, like she was still learning to talk.

"Sweetie, look at this rotting Hillbrow of ours. The first time I came here it was very beautiful and very clean. Then we moved in, black people moved in, and so the rotting came."

Matome cuts in, "That is a question of the economics of living – it doesn't have anything to do with black pride and black love."

"Matome, let me put it to you this way. This very Hillbrow that you and I are living in was cleaned by blacks back in the days. Underline blacks. Blacks were cleaning it very well, excellently, actually, and the very same black people are still cleaning it to this day. Why are they not cleaning it better today? Are you going to say it's a question of economics? Is cleaning a city a question of economy?"

"No blacks own any buildi-"

"Matome, the question on the table is not who owns the buildings or Hillbrow. It's cleaning the city that we are talking about here."

"Molamo, that in itself plays a major role."

"In the cleaning of the city, no, and if you don't have anything intelligent to say, lucifer, shut up, please."

"If some black people are not cleaning the city well, you think that means we don't have black love and pride?" Lerato asks.

"Lerato, please don't join the politics of this room." Modishi tries to stop her from getting mixed up in our politics, but she continues anyway with that sweet voice.

"Modishi, I'm just saying that we do love ourselves."

"Sweetie."

But Molamo continues: "If a black man shits in the corner of a building, is that a question of economics? Maybe. But, Matome, when black people take to shitting in every corner of Hillbrow, is it still the result of economics? Or is it a question of love and pride?"

"So, you are saying it is a question of pride?"

"Satan, I was asking you. Is it?"

Now the Zulu-boy stands up, taking a stand, these Zulu boys are like that: "I understand what Molamo is saying. How can it be that blacks were and are still cleaning this city but it is rotting today? We black people are the majority of city cleaners the world over, but we can't clean our very own city. Why? Because a black man doesn't have even a tiny amount of respect for another black man. Look at how clean Sandton and all the other white suburbs are and no white man cleans there, they are cleaned by our very own black people. If we all moved to Sandton today, I give us four weeks only and it will all look like this."

"Thank you, brother, at least you are on my side," Molamo says, smiling, and they shake hands.

"I'm not on your side, satan, just saying the honest truth, which I can see."

But Matome continues, "We are very happy people; we love and respect each other very much. But –"

"But –" the Zulu-boy cuts him, like a hunter with a rifle waiting for the right moment to take down a lion, and Matome stops.

"Say your mind, Matome."

"Let me just shut up, it's useless to try to convince you."

"There is nothing you can say that will convince us, just say your mind and let us put it straight for you. Pedi-boy, if you and your kind had even a tiny amount of love and respect, six grown-up men of your kind would not have raped a three-month-old baby."

Molamo cuts in, "Zulu, the other five were wrongfully accused, only one did that to the baby."

"Ja! I can understand why Hillbrow is rotting; we live here, we don't own anything here and we are on our way out, but I don't understand how a grown man can rape a three-month-old baby."

The Zulu-boy is not playing any more. There are tears of anger in his eyes. He pauses and looks at Matome, "We just don't have any respect for ourselves as individuals, as people and as a nation. Even if we have all the money in the world, we will never be happy people."

"It's the first time I have seen a Zulu man cry," Modishi observes.

"And it will be the last time too," Matome adds. "What I'm saying, Molamo, is that I have respect and love."

"Pedi-boy, you are hearing but you are not listening."

I try to finish with the topic before it gets out of hand: "Can we just try to be loving, respectful, respecting and happy, please?"

Before I can finish D'nice walks in without knocking, with Miss Lebogang in his right hand – this girl who deserves to be Miss Universe in each and every way.

"That is exactly what we have been talking about: he just marches in without knocking," says Molamo.

"Knock, knock."

"That's not the door, lucifer."

"You could have said 'Come in.' Hey! Lucifer, be happy, smile, Miss Lebo is here."

Lebogang hugs Matome. "How are you doing, sweet honey?"

"That is it," says D'nice. "You can only hug Matome, not these perverts, just say 'hi' to them, don't even shake their hands."

With the arrival of D'nice, we start the never-ending war that always ends with hangovers, courtesy of that Isando god. After the first sips, Lerato, who was talking to Miss Lebogang, starts it all off again: "Lebo, do you think black people are unloving, unself-respecting and unhappy people?"

"Well. Why do you say that?"

They could have kept it to themselves.

"That is a very serious question and people will hate you for whatever answer you give."

"But what do you think?"

"I don't know. D?" she asks D'nice, in that voice that knows nothing. "D?"

He looks at her, smiling.

"Are blacks unloving, unself-respecting, angry people?"

"Yes."

"Yes?"

"Yes, we are very angry, unloving people with no self-respect."

"Why?" Lerato asks.

"Look around, Lerato. You don't even have to ask. Is there anything to be happy about here?"

"I am very happy. I got this much happiness in my life."

She strokes Modishi, and D'nice says to her, "Don't lie to yourself," he mimics Molamo, "because you are not lying to me, you can't lie to me."

"D'nice, I'm very happy with myself." She pauses. "Got no reason to be unhappy."

She should have stopped there.

D'nice pauses and looks at them, at Modishi and Lerato.

"Lerato, you are a very unhappy young woman."

"I got no reason whatsoever to be unhappy."

"Do you want me to pick one thing to prove that you are a very unhappy individual, like all of us here?"

She allows him to do that. "Say it."

D'nice looks at her as if not willing to pick out the bad thing about this sister.

"You are still thinking, but I'm telling you right now that I'm very happy with what Lerato is."

He looks at Modishi, as if waiting for him to object, then he looks down and licks his lips before shattering her with the truth.

"You had two abortions, so don't tell me that you are a happy individual. One who has two abortions does not look to me like a happy someone. A happy someone, a loving, self-respecting someone cannot do that twice in one year."

He pauses as tension builds and everybody looks at him, waiting for him to continue.

"I am very sorry, Lerato. Sorry, Modishi, to cut open that scar once again. Sorry to say any of it, but Aids is killing us. Africa is the first on the list of the infected, first on the list of famine, first with mass murders and crime. Then our very own black brother raped a three-month-old baby."

Molamo nods in agreement. D'nice is preaching the bad news.

"Oh! Did I forget?" He pauses.

"What?"

"Molamo got shot. Bullets were shot into a crowd of black people who were having fun. Shot through his back, missing his spine by an inch and his kidney by even less. He nearly died from loss of blood. Why? Did you ever ask yourself why a black person would point a gun into a crowd of black people and shoot? We will never know the true reason why whoever it was did that, but don't we all really know why? We know deep in our hearts, we all really know why."

He pauses again, to give us time to think about the reasons.

"Did you all notice something when we got to the Johannesburg Hospital?"

"No."

"Molamo, did you feel anything except for the pain and the anger?"

"Nothing."

"You were smiling and crying at the same time. The worst part was that you were relaxed, as if you didn't want to live any more. Why? Because it could happen to any of us, we see it happening every day. Walk

94

around Hillbrow and you are bound to find a red map, where some-one, probably a black man, died. We have come to expect it, come to accept that my day is coming too. Do you remember what you kept saying?"

The Zulu-boy mimics Molamo: "They got me, they got me this time, motherfuckers, they got me this time."

"Because he was running away from that day, hoping it would never come. You can't blame it on politics, apartheid or economics. It is the people themselves, they don't have self-love, self-respect, and that turns into anger and hate."

A voice deep inside me says: *It is angry love.*

The darkie brother, our very own brother, shot Molamo for nothing at all. It was a Friday like this one and the weekending was in full swing. It was dark, but still early by Hillbrow standards, and the streets were full of Hillbrow life. It was month end and almost everybody had some Titos. We will never understand why, but then this is life and there are many things that we don't have answers for.

Then D'nice continues with the bad news. "What do we have to be happy for, Lerato? Give me one thing that we have to be happy about."

He pauses, looking at Lerato.

"There is nothing we have to be happy about, Lerato. Because, in the only Book God has on His green earth, it says that we are the tail of this life. Why do you think where we are living always turns into dirt? The Bible says we are the tail right after the anus. Ours is a dead life that we are living."

He's preaching now, and there is nothing that we can say, only listen and hear the truth.

"Well. I'm scaring you? Don't be scared. We are the people of all times. We were here before time started, Ali told Molamo that. The scientists too can tell you that the ancestors of humans originated in Africa, but they can't tell you that they were black, because that would be like an admission that black people are the base of all life. And let me tell you a secret that no scientist will ever tell you: black is the primary colour in this life. Burn anything – it turns black because that is its primary state. There was blackness before the sun and after the sun there will be blackness again."

That's D'nice. I never thought that he knew the Bible, but once, after he had quoted from this scripture, I went to the library and read and reread the passage. Then I confronted him.

"They are talking about Jews in the scripture, not blacks."

"Fool! Listen, it's a two-way street: the Jews do this, there is a reward for doing it and the others get the other part."

Then I had to reread again and again.

Now we are drowning a little deeper, courtesy of that great god of Isando. The funny thing is that for the whole week we didn't have enough money to buy food. Funny: We would say that we don't have money and the landlord's slaves can even cut the power to 207 sometimes. But, hey! Come Friday, we are going to drown, courtesy of that great god of Isando. He quietly searches you and you will take out the last of your money without even complaining, he is that smooth. Then comes Sunday, when we have hangovers and very hungry stomachs, courtesy of that great god of Isando, but a voice in me quotes from the book of the good God: *Let them drink and forget their misery.*

Then we continue drinking until D'nice's friends come to pick him up and take him to better parties, with that killing our rhythm, and then it's not long until the Zulu-boy takes his leave of our haven with his Zulu warriors to further their war with Isando. And then Modishi and Lerato toggle in the big bed.

"Ah! People, I'm sleeping. Good night."

Matome sinks into the single bed, resting his hard-hustling bones.

"Baba, the streets are calling you too."

"I can't hear them."

Molamo calls his well-chosen beauties to come and take him out. Then I also respond to the call of the streets. Matome heard them calling me. I'm lying to myself, saying that I'm saving some cash, not willing to spend any more of the Titos, but this six-speed gear lever keeps reminding me that it too needs some . . . and this time it was wishing for that one on Hospital Street in Dudley Heights. I don't know why it thinks about her every time I'm drowning.

* * *

I'm drunk now and I fear no evil. It's midnight. I am on my way there. Dudley Heights. No visitors after half-eleven but I am going there to get in, believe me.

These security guards, they are annoying sometimes – well, most of the time. But when I've been drinking with this god of Isando you can put Miss Universe here and, I tell you, give me thirty-seven minutes and if she was wearing a G-string I'll have it on my head. I'm that smooth.

These security guards. I greet them, trying hard not to show them that I am drunk, which they can obviously see.

"I have a problem."

"What is your problem?"

"My problem is a very manly problem."

"Hey! Talk! What is your problem? We don't have all night."

They are Zulu men and they get impatient all the time.

"Actually, I have two problems, two very manly problems." I hold out four fingers, making it seem like I wanted to say four. "Only two."

"Hey, hey! Man, you want to talk? You are wasting our time."

They are getting angry now, but that's our world, it's very angry.

"My second problem I can solve, it's already solved; it is only a problem because of the first one. If I didn't have this first problem, it wouldn't be a problem at all."

They look at me from behind the bars with anger burning in their eyes. They are Zulus, let me remind you, and they can hear I'm not Zulu. My Zulu is not that good.

"Talk, man!"

Like the Zulu-boy they only give commands.

"My first problem, the problem that I can't solve, but that I can only ask you humbly to help me with," I kneel and put my hands together, "is you, you are my first problem."

As I'm kneeling down they laugh, which is exactly what I wanted them to do – to be human.

"Hey! This boy is dead drunk. Boy, are you drunk?"

"Yes, you are right; those boys, they buy me beer and make me drink."

They are dying with laughter.

"My mother knows that I don't drink, she said that I must respect alcohol and women because they are not good. She is a woman, I respect her and she is good, very good. The alcohol, how can I respect alcohol, tell me that? Tell me, how can one respect alcohol?"

"And where is your mother?"

"Up north, she is dead now, God rest her poor soul and loving heart."

I am killing them. They are trying to control themselves, but they are dying with laughter, which is what I wanted them to do. For a moment they calm down and one of them asks, "We are your problem? This boy!"

98

They are now pretending to be angry and powerful again, but they have laughed and I have seen their back teeth.

"My boy, you are saying we are your problem, why are we your problem?" one of them asks again.

"Because I am aroused."

To accelerate the comedy I pull it out and show it to them.

They explode with laughter and one even gets out of his uncomfortable chair to get a better laugh.

"Because I'm very, very aroused, people."

"Hey! Boy, talk very carefully, you'll get hurt. We are your problem because you are aroused, talk very carefully, put it carefully or you'll get hurt. You are not Zulu, are you?"

"I'm not."

"What are you?"

"Sotho."

"Talk!"

Now we are being very diplomatic. I tell my full story and they call her through the intercom just to make sure she's there and she knows who I am. Then I'm in and they didn't even ask for an ID book or any form of identification.

The lifts here are still in working condition, which is good because I'm going to the fourteenth floor and if they weren't working I would get there tomorrow afternoon.

One of the security guards decides to walk with me to make sure I get to the right room. He has good reason for doing that, but, in truth, he enjoyed the smooth talk. And he has an idea of how the female species feel after having been lied to.

* * *

You really want to know what happened on the fourteenth floor?

It wasn't like the last time I was here with you. It was . . . Why this six-speed thing would think of her?

I have a pillow talk with beauty as she drifts off to sleep and then I look at her. It crosses my mind that if I ever tie the knot it won't be with her.

Let me give you a sure-fire way to cure a hangover that I learned from D'nice. It works, believe me: before you sleep drink a litre of cold water. I go to the kitchen to do just that. The roaches here are chasing their own dreams; they are everywhere like this place is a roach farm and for as long as I can remember she's been battling to end them. She kills the ones here, but, unfortunately, the neighbours aren't bothered by them so they always come back.

I make my way out onto the balcony and have a quick look at the city with its lights and then a thought arrives, a thought about it without lights. Pause. I hold that thought there. I don't want to think about it. Then I sit on the collapsible chair – when collapsed it resembles a drunk D'nice. I put my legs up on the short wall and have a smoky religious connection with Jah, opening the door just a little bit with bad intentions. She wakes up and . . .

I have had enough, at least for now.

* * *

I leave her with her beauty still sleeping. It is after four. I leave everything there feeling more than alive, feeling fully satisfied with this life. I just get up and walk out of the door butt naked, playing with my keys in my right hand. Freedom does not get freer than this. I am just me, not what I'm pretending to be or what I want to be. I am just me and complete.

"Hau! Hau! Madoda, what happened to you now!"

100

These security guards, they are annoying, I told you. I just smile and point for them to open the gate for me. They try to talk to me, but I'm not diplomatic any more.

"What did the woman do to you? Hau! Madoda, mhlolo ka Jesu."

I didn't care any more, I just kept pointing at the gate until they opened it in pure amazement.

In the streets I kept singing Jervis Pennington's curtain-closing tune, "Scribble", over and over again, way out of tune and loudly as well. That was a dreamer's show.

It's cold but I'm feeling very hot and more than happy. A police car pulls over, the first time ever, and I keep walking while they drive next to me. They find me amusing; all seven of them try to talk to me at the same time.

"What happened to you?"

"You got robbed?"

"Are you mad?"

"Talk to us, we are here to help you."

These police, I get robbed and they come after three years. Now that I'm having some quality time with myself they want to help me. I stop, look at them, just smile and keep singing the dreamer's hope. After a while they've had enough and then they move on to do their policing business, hopefully where it's needed.

This nakedness thing, sometimes I wish I could do it during the day and just feel the sun burning on my skin, but I always hold that thought, unwilling to grace the front pages of our daily papers with my six-speed gear lever, but this is real freedom, I can tell you.

I get into 207, drink some more water and sleep, this time some real sleeping.

* * *

Saturday. I wake up at about twelve-forty. Except for Matome and D'nice everyone is here: Modishi and Lerato on the double bed, the Zulu-boy and Ntombifuthi on the single bed, and Molamo and I on the sponge. Not that everyone is sleeping. No, they are just waiting for the right time to get up and wash before they are on their way out again. That's the streets – you never get enough of them.

I pull out a book, a Zimbabwean book, *Zabela: My Wasted Life*, go into the bathroom and soak myself, living her wasted life in the lines.

Then my Zaïrian friend, Joseph, gets in and before he can say a thing the Zulu-boy asks him, "Lekwerekwere, what do you want? Didn't I tell you I don't want to see your kind here?"

"Me no greet, me greet first: good day everybody, you still sleeping? It's two already."

"Ja, we know the time. What the fuck do you want?"

"Me visiting."

"Me visiting, me visiting; get your fucking Zaïrian ass out of here and I don't want to say that again."

The Zulu-boy, he doesn't like makwerekwere. The best part of it is that he was the one talking about black pride yesterday.

Joseph can feel the anger in his tone and see it in his eyes and, not willing to fight, he waits for me outside.

He has been a friend of mine since long ago, during that time when we were staying at Kgole'setswadi. He is a sad story all on his own. At least the present was perfect. The Zulu-boy can hurl whatever foul language he can muster, Joseph has seen too many hailstorms in his life to get upset about it; he still manages to smile, but my nakedness disturbs him. "Put on some clothes. Go put on some clothes, people are moving up and down here."

"You are not gay, are you? Am I making you feel somehow?"

102

"No. I'm no gay, but go put on clothes."

"So? What?"

He wanted to go to Mozambique to continue our search for a very secretive product called red mercury. We went there once with Ntokozo, a friend of mine I went to high school with, because he knew an old man who had the stuff there – they were related somehow. Ntokozo had newspaper cuttings that were all about red mercury, but we never had a chance to go there to pick it up and sell it to the right people, and so that dream faded until I crossed paths with Joseph.

Then together we had to search for Ntokozo and, after three days, we found him and headed for Mozambique in search of red mercury.

Crime pays, believe me, but only when you aren't caught. I was a very different person then and I'm a very different person now. So, this time, I say no; these African brothers. They are too business-minded, in the corrupt sense, and they understand the law and its loopholes – they know what they want, they know how to get it and get around the obstacles. If you are not careful they will manipulate you and leave you with a real mess to sort out.

I have been friends with Joseph for too long to be sucked in again. This guy changes cars every day but he never works. He lives glamour. He always has cash to spend. Molamo says he is a very good example of the reason why all African economies crumble. Joseph had a mansion in Bryanston, and let me tell you now that it is not true that he ran away from hunger and civil war.

Molamo said that the money that people like Joseph are using to support their glamour is stolen from their governments. If you were to search into his past, you'd find out that he is a cousin of Mobutu Sese Seko or an in-law of General Sani Abacha, here in Johannesburg spending half of the national budget.

If Mobutu once made it to the second richest man in the world, what does that make the Mobutus that are still with us? They're not living anywhere in the DRC, I can tell you that.

* * *

Believe me when I say that Matome rises to every occasion. He came back to 207, this time answering not only my rumbling stomach but all our rumbling stomachs – with a chicken, five loaves of bread and two two-litre bottles of soft drink.

Lerato looks at her man, Modishi, and thinks that he is the only man, and she slowly puts on a smile that just gets to Molamo.

"Did you see how she smiled? She's thinking bad things about you, Modishi. Don't kill the Baptist because even though he is annoying, we love him."

"Why would I kill my man? I love him."

Then why did you kill his seeds? a voice in me asks her, but for me to ask will be to kill the fun here.

"Modishi, she is going to kill you one day, I am telling you."

"If love kills then you are in danger, my ultimate man."

"Why? Lerato, why do you say that?" Molamo's voice changes; he isn't interested in what Lerato is going to say any more. He looks around for his book, as if the time is right to take the minutes, and Lerato hesitates, unsure of her answer.

"Because he loves me."

Molamo claps his hands slowly as Modishi protects Lerato, "Please, sweetie, don't talk to the ghetto intellectuals."

* * *

After we have eaten we start talking because we're full.

104

Matome tells me that my girlfriend called him this morning, asking about me; she was scared and crying: "Matome, I don't know what happen to him."

She had looked for me everywhere, even under the bed and in the closet – my phone, wallet and clothes were still at her place.

Just then, D'nice walks in, saying, "It's confirmed. It is confirmed!"

"What is confirmed?"

He goes into the bathroom, takes off his shirt, opens the tap and lets water run into the basin. He washes his head and his armpits, then he lets his trousers hang around his knees and washes his manhood.

"It's confirmed!"

"What is confirmed?"

"It is confirmed that I love women."

He takes off his trousers and puts on clean underwear, looks at the trousers carefully and then puts them back on. Changes his shirt then puts on some cologne. He looks at himself in the big mirror as Molamo asks, "Can you rephrase that, please?"

"It is confirmed that I love women."

"You mean you are not gay or . . .?"

"Fuck you!"

Then he is out to reconfirm.

Then I suddenly remember that it is my fiancée's birthday. I ask Matome to give her a call and wish her a very happy birthday and a wonderful New Year, with nothing but words.

Once, years ago, I sent her a rose on her birthday, which she took, smiling and happy, and with which she put on an act, like they do on television.

"Beautiful! For me? Thank you."

That was necessary, as the rose was bought in a town 126 kilometres away from the farm where it grew and was taken care of till it reached her hand.

I said, "This rose, my fiancée, represents my love for you."

She put it in some water, but time did it harm and it withered. Then she came back to me with the withered rose and looked at me and said, "'This rose, my fiancée, represents my love for you.' Is that what you said? Is this still representing it? Is this how your love for me will end?"

"No."

Learned one thing about my fiancée: if you have to give her a thing it must be consumable. Every thing consumable she will consume and enjoy the fact that it satisfies her. That's why I asked Matome to call her, because even if the elites of this world bought her whatever it is that is important to her in this life, other than this life, it will be second to the words.

I remember once, when it was my birthday, I reminded my father of it: "Dad, it is my birthday today."

"Oh! Son, this is the day that you gave your mother real pain and made her cry out loud. Ah! This means you are growing up, son. Grow up, son, but don't remind your mother about it, you will remind her of the pain and that is not good, son. You don't remind others of their pain and expect them to be happy about it."

That was my father and from that day I forgot the day I was born and never cared about it – it's just a day like any other day. Sometimes I think that my father was a Zulu. A Zulu boy reminds his father that it's his birthday and his father says, "Hau! This is the day you were born. Grow, grow up, my boy, then you can go to Johannesburg and drive a taxi."

But that's my father too, he too grew up without celebrating birthdays or caring about the day that he was born; he never even noticed when it came and went, why would he start now?

* * *

Miss Lebogang and Lerato are in our haven, Molamo, D'nice and I are the only ones with them. Matome, the Zulu-boy and Modishi are serving the Titos, helping some wannabe artist in the downtown studios.

There are six books on my left; all of them are opened back up on the wooden floor. I have a pen and paper and am writing down my thinking and not minding everybody else.

D'nice is playing chef, trying to do everything in a quarter of the usual time as he has some appointment to attend at eight and he had calculated that at ten-to he'd have to leave 207.

He finishes.

"Satan, if you are hungry, you can help yourself."

"Lucifer, please put my share on a plate and then I will definitely help myself because you can't help me with that."

"Please, you people must stop cursing each other. Why do you always have to curse when talking? It is not a good thing."

Miss Lebogang is speaking her mind, trying to impose her ways on us. D'nice doesn't curse that much, but he curses me as he is serving the food: "Fuck you, I'm not your wife."

"D, please stop cursing."

"Lucifer, I don't have a wife and I will never have one."

He puts the food on the plate and Lerato asks, "Can I come with you?"

"No."

Then they are out.

When I think of cursing I think that it is simply people connecting with each other. They have lost their personal space and when they share their personal space then cursing becomes a way out.

For example: you wake up in the early morning because Modishi is making love to Lerato. Or, you are woken by the track "Ooh! Aah!" from the album *Love Anthems*, as D'nice is fiddling with Miss Lebogang the best way he knows how. Not to mention the fact that Matome walks around this place naked every morning, like Max the gorilla, applying lotion to his body and looking at himself in the mirror. And then Lerato will do the same thing with the comment, "There is nothing you don't already know."

True. I know the frontier, but she is still an unexplored frontier to me and you. And you have to look at her because, if you don't, it is going to be a big joke, and Matome will look at you and say, "If only you can see yourself with my eyes, baba."

The second time she did it, Molamo couldn't take it. "You should stop doing that, Lerato."

"Molamo . . ."

"No, don't Molamo me. I'm not challenging you to an argument here. I'm telling you to stop getting naked in front of us all because we are not all Modishi and you are not my girlfriend."

"Molamo, control your animal instincts. Don't let them control you!"

That was Matome, blowing the whole thing into a big joke.

"Don't say a thing, Matome, you can't tell me anything when it comes to this."

"Handle yourself, brother, that's all I'm telling you."

Why does she do that? Because she's lost her sense of privacy and personal space; to her whether we're there or whether we're not makes no difference.

* * *

It's Sunday.

Forget about going to church, it's a day to relax, heal hangovers and, if it comes to it, get drunk again. Matome is the only one who ever visits the holy house. The last time I was there both my grandparents were still breathing.

Now all I have left to do this particular Sunday is to have a real sleep. I wake up around half-five and have a long, hot bath, living somebody's wasted life through the lines.

By eight the female species are all gone and the kangaroo court is in session. The weekend is in review. Matome, who never says a thing about himself, is heading it.

Molamo is, as always, interested in everything – he is the only one who gains much out of this kangaroo thing. He won't write anything down now though; he'll wait until we are all asleep, then he'll take out his scribble and write down what he found interesting and important.

Modishi will sometimes love a line; he'll repeat it twice, then he'll take out his self-made diary to jot it down. I call his diary the Modishi enigma, because if you can read it and understand it then you will nearly understand all that Modishi is.

The Zulu-boy has one too, but it doesn't work like Modishi's.

D'nice only listens or talks.

Here, lies and half-lies, truth and half-truth, observations and conclusions are all on the table, but the weekend is gone and done with and all we can do is hope for a better one next time around.

Then, after the kangaroo court, there are a few things that I have to write about, but first I take a midnight nap. I'm not sleeping, it's a nap to clear out my thinking. Maybe I can still do some work.

* * *

I wake up after three.

I wake up after three every Monday morning, then I lie on the sponge, thinking. It has become a routine to me. Even if, as they say, Hillbrow doesn't sleep, I can guarantee you that it will be asleep by this time on a Monday morning.

I will think about the weekend, think about me, just reflecting and smiling to myself, or I will think of something from or about the weekend that will push me to pen my thinking.

This morning I feel like going out of our fortress. I go down to the security checkpoint in some sandals and trunks. When I get there he is sleeping, the security guard, and the gates are locked.

I wake him up, disturb his uncomfortable sleep, in Matome's tone. He likes Matome: "Baba, I want to get out and you are sleeping, baba."

He wakes up, annoyed and thinking about the harm he could do me. But there is nothing he can do but open the gate.

"Where are you going? And when are you coming back?"

"Coming back now."

I walk to the twenty-four-hour supermarket to get myself some cold water and a soft drink. Here, some of Hillbrow is still alive and refusing to die. A few brothers lean against a car in the street, I'm thinking that they have money but are bored. The street prescription doctors are still here as well and they think that I need some relief from this life and they present themselves. I give them my thumb, "Ke sharp."

I don't know why but I'm singing Jervis Pennington's tune, "How do you know when you are happy", way out of tune but not loud. At the door of the supermarket there is a pack of street children sniffing glue and just generally being busy with being street children. I just act like I can't see them and they do the same for now, but when I get out they want some change, which they get with the slip as well.

110

Back in the street an emergency rescue vehicle comes running down Claim and I can't fight the thought that another dreamer just bit the dust somewhere somehow.

Then I'm back. He didn't lock the door so I just open it and get in.

"Lock the door," he says.

And I respond, "Isn't it part of your job description? Because I'm not working here."

I lock the thing, take a seat and look into his angry eyes.

"What I have experienced in this world is that if one hates you, you tend to hate them back; but if they love you, you love them back. If they accept you, you accept them back. Am I right or wrong?"

I pause and he looks at the wall.

"Because I think you don't like me much and that is why I don't like you much. Do you know that I don't like you? And that is because you don't like me at all."

I pause.

He looks at me, but I'm looking at him and my eyes are not going anywhere. Then he looks into the distance.

"But, true, I don't have a reason to dislike you and maybe you have one big reason to dislike me, but I don't have a reason to dislike you."

I'm still looking at him, holding my breath, hoping that maybe we can have peace. But peace is something that hasn't come to him yet.

Then I get up.

"It is a very beautiful Monday morning, cold and chilly, but beautiful. Don't miss it, please."

I was trying to end our cold war, but I knew that he only had hate for me. People have that. They just hate you for nothing, but don't let it get you down because somewhere you too hate someone for no apparent reason.

Then I'm back in this haven. Molamo is on the sponge, D'nice on the single bed, Modishi, Matome and the Zulu-boy sharing the big bed.

You know, people are funny when they are sleeping; some are beautiful to look at, some are just too scary to even steal a look at. Then I laugh, thinking of all the things that are beautiful about life.

I drift off into a thinking-sleep.

I wake up on a real Monday morning.

"People, it's Money-day morning today," Matome will tell you after he has pushed his sexy legs into some sandals and visited the bathroom. "It's Money-day morning and we are here to work."

And he will bang the decaying door, not to offend you in your sweet sleep but to remind you of all your reasons for being here.

Helen
of
Troy

Ntombifuthi

Well, let's be honest, the average Hillbrowean has never seen the thong of a single lekgosha because the average Hillbrowean has average morals. Come to Hillbrow in the early morning and take a look at the customers and you will see that they are definitely not from Hillbrow.

Why do you think that these girls are doing this?

This is a billion-rand industry. The advertising people will tell you that sex sells. I know it sells.

Honestly, I have never taken out my hard-earned rands and bought a condomed round. No. We had it for free, courtesy of Matome. He talked to them, teased them, made them smile and bought them beer or something special when they didn't even expect it. To Matome, they were sisters living a hard life, and the fact that they did it smiling, gave him some kind of hope. So, in time, they started visiting him and then they got acquainted with all the 207s.

"Hey! When are you going to give it to me?" I said, stroking her.

"Anytime, as long as you have the cash."

"Well, I'm a poor man, I don't have cash; with what can a poor man buy?"

"The poor are the dead."

"So I'm dead, but you can be my friend and comfort me."

"Poor men don't have friends, poor men don't fuck."

Excuse the language.

I said, "But you arouse this poor man."

"You, poor man, tell your dick not to get aroused." She said that in a very sweet tone, a tone that would get you aroused every time.

We always teased them and they always teased us back. I once asked this other one, "Where are you going to end up with this profession?" feeling, more than anything, that she didn't deserve to be doing what she was doing.

She had just told me that she was a graduate of that great institution of education and this night thing was just a thing to keep her above water. I had smiled to myself when she told me that, and she had misinterpreted that smile and decided that I didn't believe her. She ordered her friend to tell me which degree she held, but her friend said, "He doesn't believe you, so let it be."

"I don't believe her," I tried to cut her short.

Her friend continued, "Shit, who cares if you don't believe her? And fuck you! You aren't God and there is nothing you can fucking do to help either."

"Whatever!"

And, with that, her friend ended her interruption, but the next day she came with proof that she was really a graduate of Wits. She said she was still looking for a job and a work permit. She was our neighbour from Swaziland and her parents named her Ntombifuthi (a girl again). I never had any reason to talk to her about her sisters, but the Zulu-boy did ask sometime after much poking with her.

The Zulu-boy liked her, he couldn't enjoy her enough and though he had it for free the first time, courtesy of Matome, he somehow became a loyal customer.

On one particular night, he came back to the haven after eleven, had his supper and was out again. He had to relieve himself and he was thinking about the Swazi girl.

116

Afterwards he took a few breaths, recovered, and, relieved, took out the currency equivalent of the services offered.

"No, not today. I can't take your money today. Can I, instead, lie with you here in my arms?"

Locking the Zulu-boy in her arms, she felt that she had found everything she wanted in this world and that now it could pass; there wasn't anything that she wanted out of it any more. The Zulu-boy looked at her, thinking things, and she asked, "Can I kiss you?"

He smiled, thinking that he was good. No, he was perfect, to make an angel of the night feel like a woman again.

"Why?"

"I want to make love to you. I do love you."

A kiss lead to . . . and that lead to . . . and ended up as pillow talk again. They just had to talk about something.

"When I'm with you I feel loved, I can't help wanting to hold you."

Take my advice: talk shit, zip your trousers and leave, because if you don't, you will feel pity and fall in love.

Ntombifuthi was the seventh daughter of a priest. Her younger brother was here too, in Nelspruit, studying to arm himself with a survival job.

She was beautiful. I always wondered why she was passed over and, instead of being one of the many queens of Swaziland, became a Johannesburger. Now, when I think about it, I know that it was the beauty that attracted my Zulu brother and the brains came as a bonus.

This sister had her special customers. She wasn't one of the street angels, she was more of an escort – you had to call her and make reservations in advance and it was not that obvious that she was an angel of the night.

But then the Zulu-boy just started dating her and we knew right away that what we were looking at was love. And, the way we saw it, it got very serious. But she was still an angel. It was still on sale for those with rands enough, white men looking for . . .

The angels of the night all loved and worshipped Matome and Modishi, and sometimes on Sundays they would come to 207 and cook us some Sunday food, acting like they were housewives and nursing us, which I didn't like. There were four of them sharing 406; D'nice poked them all and loved to be with them, he spent most of his time tease-talking nothing-shit with them.

"Out of all the dicks that ever went in, which of them have you enjoyed most and why?"

"Yours?"

"I'm not that good."

"You don't believe in your fucking self."

Excuse the language, that's how these people talk.

"Not that I don't enjoy sex but you never know with you people; you fucking tell me, then maybe I can do it even better."

"Sex is sex, D. Men push it in and out, then in and out. There is nothing more you can do."

"You are hurting me, sweetie."

There was nothing serious you could ask these people, but they found some comfort in us and maybe love as well.

If not, then at least Ntombifuthi found something in the Zulu-boy. Love is another thing, maybe another language, but at least in Hillbrow I came across love. The Zulu-boy loved the Swazi-girl in ways that I didn't understand, but that's just how our lives are: you don't have to understand everything.

Tebogo

I read most of Molamo's writing, but Tebogo read all of it.

Once, this other man that was, I guess, a good example to the other Molamo, wanted to marry Tebogo. The first person she told was Molamo. This other brother tried and tried to push Tebogo into marriage, then one day when we were having our late-night supper she knocked on the door and walked in. Molamo looked at her and whatever she had on her mind just got deleted. The next best thing to do was to cry and that's what she did. What would you think if someone's girlfriend just came in and started to cry? Molamo thought about the other Molamo first: "What? Where is my boy?"

Funny, this man; it's at a time like this that he is suddenly concerned about his child.

"I don't know what to do."

"About?"

"Khutso."

'Oh! Your boyfriend again; what's his problem this time?"

"He wants to marry me."

"So," pause, "he wants to marry you, so what?"

Pause.

"Do you want to marry this . . .?"

Pause.

"Well, do you?"

"I don't know."

Molamo looked at her with anger and disgust.

119

"Tebogo! You're saying that to me?"

"Sorry, but I really don't know. I don't know."

He believed her – that, this time, she really didn't know.

"Didn't I warn you never to say that to me? Don't you think? You must think something about it. If you don't know, who will? Because he's not asking me to marry him."

"You tell me."

"You need my approval? He has money, yes, and he's living the life, but I don't think he's a good man for you."

A voice in me asks: *Why?* And I asked Molamo later, when we were discussing the Tebogo and Khutso saga, and got a simple, straight-to-the-point answer: "Because he can't handle her."

With that Tebogo knew for sure that one day Molamo would have to marry her.

"Call him."

She called him, asking, "What are you going to tell him?"

The black brother thought that whatever he did trying to get her to marry him worked, but Molamo could speak with power, I can tell you.

Khutso answered in total devotion, "My sweetheart."

"Khutso. How are you? You are talking to Molamo."

"Molamo?"

"Sorry to call you, brother, but I want you to do me a favour. Stay away from Tebogo, please."

"Stay away from Tebogo?"

The brother was regurgitating the news, but he recovered soon enough.

"Who are you?"

"Khutso, my name is Molamo and like I said I want you, please, to stay away from Tebogo."

"Are you threatening me?"

"No, I'm not threatening you. I'm telling you that Tebogo is my whore, excuse my language, but she is my whore and I want you to stay away from her."

There was a pause as Molamo let the shocking news sink in.

"Now, she is a whore?"

"I said excuse my language, please. She is a whore to me and please, please, leave my whore alone. Once again excuse the language."

"Who are you?"

"Molamo."

"Molamo?"

"Yes. I was only delivering a message, brother, I'm not fighting, so please do as I ask you or we will have to talk face to face, excuse the cliché. I'm sorry if I disturbed you, excuse me."

It sounded to me like it was a scene he had rehearsed, a scene from one of his many scripts, but believe me it was live.

"Don't worry about him any more," he said to Tebogo, and they walked out of 207. Those two, Molamo and Tebogo, you would wish . . .

He was back just as soon. This guy believed in himself when it came to Tebogo. Tebogo needed a man and she found him in Molamo. There was too much of Molamo in her mind for her to ever recover and have feelings for another man. They were both having other relationships openly and they liked to believe that they were, had, something-something that I don't really have a clear description for, only that this was Tebogo the lawyer-girl and her man, Molamo, the hustler-poet, and who could break that kind of a union?

The Zulu-boy told Molamo once, "You are one lucky lucifer, to have a woman as loving and caring as Tebogo."

"You Zulus don't know women. You don't understand how to handle a woman, you only see the outside, you instil fear in them and then you think that they love and respect you. A woman is more than sex, more than beauty, more than curves. Ask me, I have an idea; I know what her inner self looks like and you would not love it."

The Zulu-boy gave him a look and stopped because you couldn't argue with Molamo. He was a natural liar and that was why he was such a perfect writer: he lied. If you ever listened to him he'd get into your system and then you'd need him like Tebogo did. A voice inside me says: *You will lose her one day when you need her the most, and even the great god of Isando won't be able to help you then.*

Tebogo's mind was Molamo's colony; she listened to him too much, read too much of his writing. She'd say to him, "I don't have anything to read, have you anything that I can read?"

He'd look at her and write a poem there and then, a poem especially for her. Molamo understood Tebogo, knew how to pull her strings, just as he knew when not to; and you too know and understand your woman, don't you? You can say things that sound very uncaring and untender to her. How lucky some of us bastards are.

Tebogo was Molamo's first girl and she's still Molamo's. They started school together and from that first day his heart took a place in Tebogo's body and Tebogo's heart became Molamo's. They have being living in each other since.

Her father was a very strict man. He guarded his three daughters like a female ostrich guarding its nest, but she had to leave. She had to leave the ostrich nest to go far away to get higher education. Molamo was there and he took full advantage and then a baby boy cried. Tebogo named him Molamo before he even took his thirtieth breath of this contaminated air. Her mother named him Sentsho. But we all called him Molamo; Sentsho was just his second name.

122

They were the two Molamos in Tebogo's life. Maybe one was on the left and the other on the right.

How could she ever recover?

Lerato

The first time I was introduced to Lerato I was dead drunk. I had just come back from streeting the streets. I got home long after six and found this beautiful girl in my haven.

"You are not . . ."

The words would not come out, they'd got stuck somewhere, I don't know where. Then I sat down and the alcohol just left me.

"Let me sleep, I will talk to you when I wake up."

Then I just fell on the double bed and was asleep in a wink and that became the big joke that week.

She was that beautiful; I don't like to impress people and so I don't get easily impressed, but her beauty was another thing. She was born in the suburbs of western Johannesburg, where her mother had been a maid all her life. Lerato didn't have any family other than her mother and the white family that adopted her. She told Modishi that she had never visited any relatives, ever. All she knew was that her mother was a Xhosa, but they never talked much about it because her mother didn't care about it. She had her mother and they had their adopted family.

For a suburb girl Lerato was amazing. At first I thought she was from somewhere-somewhere in Soweto. She was a totally different creature, tall with very firm curves. At fifteen she looked like she was twenty-one, and if you talked to her you'd think that you were talking to a twenty-three-year-old intern with the world as her playground.

Modishi's one and only Lerato.

How did a Windsor girl get to know Modishi?

Wherever they met, her heart told her that Modishi was the one she was looking for and she took his heart, which he gave willingly. On his part he never stopped to consider a future beyond her. For Modishi, after Lerato, there was no other woman that he could make love to.

Molamo thought of her as the ultimate high-class whore; she could fit everywhere perfectly, she knew what to say and how to say it. He ran into her a couple of times with the other men in her life and, on every occasion, they happened to be white boys.

Now, let me tell you something: Molamo hated white people. He worked with them and could share a smile, even a dinner table, with them, but deep down he had no respect for them.

Although nothing was said the facts remained. When Sunday came with its kangaroo court, the honourable Matome presiding, Molamo asked us, "If you have a friend, a dear and wonderful friend, who loves this girl with all his heart and this girl is cheating on him, do you think you should tell him?"

At the time we all knew that the question was directed at Modishi. I ventured an opinion, which was that it was better to know, and then Modishi said, "No. I wouldn't tell. He'll have to see it for himself. What you saw might be an ex-boyfriend or a friend, and even if you caught them in the act, it might not be the way you think it is. People like to have casual sex. I wouldn't tell because it's none of my business."

Molamo tried to convince Modishi of the advantage of being told of things like this, but he still couldn't see it.

"The Baptist, don't you think it is better to know the truth than to be left in the dark?"

"You could tell him, but if you just let it be it will eat away at her inside and she will confess, eventually, because other relationships are only sex, nothing more. So, if I were you, I wouldn't destroy their union. Let it be, and if it ever ends, let it not be because of you."

"But if it were me, I would like you to tell me."

"Molamo, you can't trust people. I'm here now, in 207, and where is Lerato? I can only assume where she is. Because even if I tell her that she owes me an explanation, then, after the explanation, what? Because you either have to live with the explanation or your friend's story."

"I think it is an advantage to know."

"Molamo, you're having casual sex with other men's girls; even worse, you are having sex with other men's wives. Do you think that they would like to know about that? And, if they knew, do you think that they would remain husbands? Do you want Nolizwe's man to know that you are having sex with the mother of his children?"

"Modishi, it is good to know."

"Now, I have a feeling that you want to tell me something about Lerato – don't tell me, please."

"No. It's far away from you and Lerato. Just that I know who Tebogo is fucking and I can live with that. I would rather know."

Modishi looked at him and he smiled.

"Your problem is that you think I am stupid. And let me be stupid to you. I can see, think and respond to any situation in the way that suits me, and I don't want to respond to my life in your way. I'm very comfortable with everything I am. Lerato, she's the only whore, as you always refer to them, that I'm fucking. And, somewhere inside me, I believe that I'm the only one fucking her. But maybe that statement has its flaws. Maybe you know better. But in my mind I'm the only one fucking her and I don't want to know who she has fucked or is fucking, thank you."

126

Whores and fucking: that was the first and the last time I heard a curse come out of Modishi the Baptist's mouth. But then I believe that if they give you a name, you become that name.

Basedi

The doctor called long after we had forgotten about her. And we had thought Molamo's talk of dating a doctor was just poverty talk!

It was a private number and unlike other people, who don't like to answer private numbers, I answer them with hope. I just say, "Hello." I don't say my name because the other person, can I say she, because it was a she this time, knows who she is trying to call. If it's a wrong number, she will just have to go without any idea of who she was talking to.

"Hi, I'm Basedi. Can I please talk to Molamo?"

"Basedi from where?"

"I'm his friend."

"He has never talked about you before."

Excuse me if I was being rude, but I wasn't in the habit of giving away people's information to Basedis over the phone, especially when the individual they are looking for has his own cellphone. I wanted to know who she was first and why she didn't have Molamo's phone number, and, most importantly, why we had never heard about her before.

"I admitted him at the hospital some time ago when you brought him in."

"Oh! Hello, Basedi."

"Hello."

From now on she was no longer a doctor but a woman with the name of Basedi. Who cares about the doctor part? We, well, Molamo, was only interested in the woman named Basedi.

Basedi was an intern who had just turned twenty-five, with, well, put it this way: as a doctor you would have to say that she was in the wrong profession by appearance. When someone talks about a female doctor I always picture someone like Nkosazana Zuma. Well, Basedi was a doctor and opinions have to change.

Molamo was in the Johannesburg central library doing harm to some African book, harming the lines of *The Bank is my Shepherd*. He hated private numbers. It was like a phobia to him, or whatever you call it. He always changed his voice into Tebogo's and you would think that you were really speaking to a lady: "Molamo's phone, Tebogo speaking; sorry to answer his phone. Hi!"

"Hi!"

Basedi was thinking: Who is this Tebogo now? She expected Molamo to be the kind of lonely, honest man who had never had sex twice in all of his life.

"He just went out but he's coming back. Can I ask who is on the line?"

"Basedi. I was just calling to find out if he is doing fine."

Pause. Basedi. Basedi from where?

Then she felt the need to explain: "I was taking care of him when he was at the hospital, after he was shot."

"Hold on, Basedi, here he is coming."

"Thank you."

She thinks: Well, at least she isn't his girlfriend. And he said, "It's Basedi." As if it was Tebogo giving Molamo the phone.

"Basedi, this must be a very bad day."

"Why?"

"Why would a doctor call a hustler? A queen doesn't call common men."

"I'm just calling to find out if you are doing fine. I'm happy to hear your voice."

"Hmm." By that Molamo implied: you don't know what you are getting yourself into, my dear.

"It sounds to me like you are very happy, and if you're happy then I'm happy too."

"Come see me, then you'll be ecstatic. That's if your husband won't mind?"

"My husband? My husband, he won't mind at all, he's a gentleman."

"I'm at the central library reading a book."

"What kind of book are you reading?" She smiled, feeling not happy but ecstatic.

"Come and see. It's a very good book, it's African."

"African?"

"Yes, South African."

Pause, as they were getting heavy on each other, it was like they didn't want to talk any more, but somebody had to say something, they were on the line, and so Molamo advanced, "So, when do I see you?"

"When do you want to see me?"

"I want to see you now."

"Now?"

"Exactly what I said, now, and then you can see what kind of a book I'm reading."

*   *   *

Did you ever take somebody on a first date to the library? Did you ever read her your favourite novel and write her a poem in the back of the library book, both of you dating and signing it, and then put it back on the shelf so that the masses can come and read when, exactly, Molamo kissed Basedi for the first time? The book: *Maru*. The location: Johannesburg central library. Even today the book is still there, without the last page – someone took it, impressed by what the poet can do. That to you is not romantic in any way, but that was Molamo's way of doing things. .

* * *

Fiddle-fiddle makes a grown woman feel like a baby. Fiddle-frolic makes a feminine heart embrace a man. Frolic-frolic makes a queen desert queen-hood. She even came to the haven 207 together with Molamo. They played the track "You're Hurting Me (but don't Stop)" from the album *Love Anthems*. The music made Basedi say to Molamo, "Molamo, I can't live without you."

He looked at her carefully. She had just evoked a ghost from his past. "What?"

"I said I couldn't live without you."

Pause, he gave her an injured smile, then it disappeared, and she asked, "Molamo, what?"

But it was too late; she had woken up the ghost in Molamo's past: Petunia. She too had said, "Molamo, I can't live without you," touching her chest over her heart, one hand over the other, and pressing down hard. She had closed her eyes, maybe imagining the thousand pieces it had come to, then opened her hands towards him as if giving him the pieces of what had been her heart.

A long time ago he'd woken up in a single bed inherited by his father from the white people he was serving. The chains and the springs were dead and had been replaced with carved wood and an old, abused sponge. It was nowhere near comfortable, but he had learned to extract some comfort from it. It was a cold winter morning during the school holidays, so he had nowhere to go and his grandmother just let him sleep.

He wasn't aware of the commotion outside until he heard someone say, "Petunia died?"

He opened his eyes and looked at the grass roof of the hut. And then someone else said, "They say that she hanged herself yesterday night in her bedroom."

The goodbye letter was short, it read: "Molamo, I can't live without you."

You would wish you weren't alive, wish the soil would swallow you, but it won't. What is done is done, blamed or blameless, we have to keep on living.

After that he tried not to have time for the sister with the medical degree, but she kept calling and calling until, finally, she felt that she had been ignored enough.

* * *

One night, just after eleven, we were in our haven having our late-night supper and generally being ourselves. Modishi and the Zulu-boy were the only ones who weren't home; they were doing music some-where and wouldn't be back until the early hours.

Molamo's phone rang; it was a private number, so he went out onto the balcony to answer it: "Molamo's phone, hello!"

"Can I speak to Molamo, please?"

"He's not here now. Can I ask who is calling, please?"

"Basedi."

"Hi! Basedi, he has been talking about you too much lately."

"Where is he?"

"He's busy developing a film script with some of his friends."

There was a gentle knock on our door. I went to the door and peeped through the spyhole. It was blocked, someone had put their hand over it so I couldn't see who it was, but everybody did that. As I opened the door I could hear Molamo on the balcony talking in his fake Tebogo voice; he was saying, "When he is doing that he doesn't answer phones. Basically he doesn't want to be disturbed."

Molamo continued talking to the phone as the doctor calmly greeted us.

"How are you doing?" asked Matome.

She put on a smile as if to say: How can you ask me that? And he got the message and shouted, "You are busted, baba! You're busted!"

"Molamo, hi!"

Molamo turned around. There was the doctor. Sorry, Basedi, we weren't at the hospital. She was only a doctor at the hospital.

"My dear . . ." Matome put down his plate, trying to dilute the tension before it became unbearable, getting up to give her a hug. "A surprise visit and a big surprise at that. Do you know that you are the only doctor I ever gave a hug to? I hope you aren't the last."

She gave D'nice a hug, fighting to keep her cool and doing very well but I couldn't wait for the show to start. I was already holding my breath and then she turned and looked at Molamo, thinking: Where is the lady I was talking to?

A voice in me tells the sister: *He is an actor and he is going to put on a good show.*

Attention, eyes ready, and action.

"Basedi."

She looked at him with enforced calm, and then the expensive South African dam built in the mountains of Lesotho, gave way to the water.

Matome tried to spoil the fun, "Boys, let us take a walk."

133

No way, we wanted to see for ourselves, first hand, how he got out of this one because he was going to lie to us about it later, when she was gone. Matome understood our position and he took his leave of our haven.

Molamo gave her a hug.

"Basedi, I want to say I'm sorry, but I'm not sorry. You know why I did that and you know why I have to do it: you have a far bigger status than I have. I'm trying to run away from you. I'm trying not to love you to a point that I can't return from."

"What do you mean bigger status? I'm a woman and that is my status."

She was calm and her hands were expressing clearly what was coming out of her mouth, but the words and the busted dam were beginning to mix.

"Basedi, think about the future. Me, in this state, and you, in that state, having a happy future together is not at all possible. We can have a future together but it's not going to be a happy one."

There were tears coming out of her eyes. She said, "As a doctor I scare you now?"

"No, but a hustler and a doctor can never be happy together."

"You're not a hustler, you're a poet and I didn't make myself a doctor as you didn't make yourself a poet and that doesn't mean we cannot be together."

Molamo looked up, he wanted to say something but it wasn't a good thing, and that voice in me commented: *He just said: "Shit! What have I got myself into?"*

He hugged her and wiped away the water from the dam; then he hugged her again, very tight, and whispered in her ear, "Stop crying."

She whispered, "Molamo, I can't live without you."

This time he managed to smile, but those words would always wake up a ghost for Molamo. Holding her brought back the calmness, some degree of happiness, and then she smiled, becoming lighter as he was holding her. Eighteen minutes went by and if she hadn't said something it would have been longer.

"Molamo."

He was feeling the effect that he had on this woman. He didn't want to say anything, he decided to cry.

Then D'nice decided that it was time for us to go. We had seen the show, which wasn't anything like the Molamo that we were used to and D'nice concluded, on the way out of 207, "He is scared to talk to the doctor woman."

Matome was at the security checkpoint and now he wanted to know what was going on and why we had left when we did. "People, did they chase you out?"

D'nice gave it to him, inviting no more questions, "We just left because it was time to leave."

Molamo and the sister reached a conclusion and she came down alone. We walked her to her car. I was thinking, true, sometimes brains and beauty do mix and here between us is the evidence.

*   *   *

Three days later Basedi called Matome in the middle of the night and he gave Molamo the phone.

"Molamo." There was relief in her voice.

"I am the only one, on this, God's green earth. Basedi. Good very early morning to you."

"I want to talk to you now."

"I'm listening."

"I mean face to face."

"You are coming to Hillbrow?"

That was a "yes" and she drove her expensive wheels into Hillbrow again, to come and sort out her heart.

Molamo went down. The gates were already locked and the security guard on duty was sleeping with the heater on.

"Did a woman ever love you?"

With that he woke up and looked at Molamo.

"Ja! I didn't think so, but I know you have loved and wished to love many women."

"I'm having sex with women, have been long before you were born," he said, and got up to open the gate for him.

She had already parked her car in front of our fortress and Molamo called her in. The security guard wanted to lock the gate, but Molamo held it open, saying, "I'm not going anywhere but I need to talk to this lovely woman."

She got out of her car and came to Molamo.

"Basedi, make me understand."

He gave her a hug and a light kiss and she managed to smile, noticing now that Molamo was half-naked. She looked back at her car as if she was checking that it was still there. It was still there. She turned back to Molamo.

"Basedi, what do you want in life?"

"I don't know. I only knew I wanted to be a doctor and now I am."

"What do you need?"

"What do I need?"

"Yes, Basedi. What do you need in this life?"

She looked into the distance and when her eyes came back to his face he was still waiting for an answer.

"Molamo, I want you and I don't know how I can make you understand that. In my whole life I never had any need whatsoever for male
companionship. I didn't need a man at all. Well, I didn't until I met
you."

She smiled in disbelief of the fact that she had ever thought that way.
She was altering her whole world, still not able to believe that she was
saying that word: need.

This was the second time that she had told Molamo this tale and
for the second time he didn't believe it at all. No woman as beautiful
as Basedi could fan all men away from her; she was just trying to make
herself appear holy and that wasn't going to work because she threw
herself in his path.

"Molamo, I want you, I need you."

"How different are need and want?"

"I think they are the same thing, they only differ in degrees."

"Can I ask you again?"

"Please."

"Basedi, what do you want in life?"

He didn't know why he asked that question again, but he waited for
an answer because the first answer wasn't what he had been expecting.
He just held her tight, thinking: Where do I start with this business of
breaking up and breaking a heart?

Then, as there was nothing else in her mind, no other answer to that
question, Molamo pretended to cry, so as to soften it for her, so that she
wouldn't cry too much. Then he said, "Basedi, I'm going to let you go
now because I don't think we can work out, we can never be."

She felt like a twig being cut off at the base as he let her go; she had
to balance herself again and, as she looked up at him, she saw not the
eyes but the tears.

"We can be, Molamo, you just have to want to be with me and you will see that it's possible."

"You don't understand."

Molamo looked up at the concrete ceiling, trying to hide the tears, and wiped them away.

"Molamo, there is nothing to understand: I love you, you love me."

He looked into her eyes and called her name in a way that she didn't understand.

"Basedi. Basedi, you are a doctor and I am a hustler. However much we want this, a union between a hustler and a doctor won't work . . ."

"Yes, we'll make it work. You said that I was a woman before I became a doctor and let me tell you, you were a man before you became a hustler, and I need the man, not the hustler. I am a woman."

"Basedi."

She felt, suddenly, that that wasn't her name.

"Try to understand what I'm saying."

He paused and he wiped away his tears.

"Yes, we can make it work, but I have a past. I have a history and obligations and those are things that are going to stress you out."

He looked at her, trying to put on a smile, "You see, Basedi, I'm beginning to want you, and I can't want you because, even if I was to have you, in the long run we can never be happy."

He paused and looked at her to see if she had got the message.

"Molamo, I'm not expecting you to be a virgin, I'm not expecting that."

Molamo looked at her.

"Molamo, do you love me? Do you love me?"

"Basedi, that's not the thing, I think you deserve better than what I can give you."

She looked at him, thinking, if only she could open her inside and let him see for himself that she really loved him, because her words were not getting through to him.

"Molamo, I can't live without you. I cannot live without . . ."

"Don't say that. Don't ever say that."

"Molamo, I can't live without you. If I can't have you, I don't have a reason to live. This ring on my finger. I'm not married. I bought it, married myself with it, so that then I didn't have a reason to have a man in my life. There was no man man enough and every man who had any interest in me, well, the ring would tell them that I'm already taken. They respected me as a married woman, but I was married to myself. Told myself that, if I needed a child, the sperm bank was always available, but when I saw you I forgot that I married myself."

She took the ring off her finger and gave it to him.

"I divorced myself the day I first met you."

They looked at each other.

"What do I say, Molamo, to make you understand?"

She paused, then she started to cry out loud, and Molamo held her in his arms for a moment, wiping away the tears, and she calmed down until she remembered that he was still going to let her go.

She pushed him away, and ran out into the street, stopping at the car and looking back. Then she broke down again, and cried, "Molamo."

Then the words wouldn't come out any more.

They looked at each other for a moment, then she turned around and her car made a sound and the indicators lit up. He walked after her, the expensive ring dropping from his pocketless shorts, but she just looked at him while the car was idling and then wiped away her tears.

Then the tyres screeched as she made a U-turn. A hard stop at corner Claim and Van der Merwe. Then the tyres screeched again.

Basedi: True, she was married to herself before she met Molamo. Her father was each and every reason why she married herself. Although he loved her very much, he represented marital abuse to her mother. A resolution was born to be by herself and be happy alone. Then, after that, a resolution to be a doctor. She married herself to fan off men, which worked very well until her path crossed Molamo's.

Basedi kept on overwhelming Matome with hugs, although we never saw her again in our haven. Matome passed on hello's and hi's from Basedi and to Basedi. "Baba, I was with your female doctor today, she said to tell you hello."

"Tell the bitch I said hello, how are you doing? I'm doing fine and I hope she is doing very fine too."

One day, after Matome spent Friday and Saturday with Basedi, he asked, while heading the kangaroo court, "Molamo. Why did you let go of Basedi?"

"Stress."

"Aren't they all stress?"

"Not all women. Basedi is big stress. She married herself. Why? Because she is superintelligent." He looked at D'nice. "Some people are too intelligent for their own good and become social misfits."

"Fuck you. Molamo, you're the socially handicapped misfit and you can't even see that," D'nice replied.

Matome tried to dilute the situation, saying, "Molamo, she is a good girl."

"For you, Matome, but ask me, because I know what she thinks after I ejaculated in her. Maybe if you ejaculate in her you will understand."

"I like her."

"Have her. I played my part very well, thank you. If I didn't, well, I feel I did and I am satisfied."

Hard
Living

———

Money-day

The sun rises from the east side. I know that, but you hardly ever see the sun rising here. Every morning this other building covers ours with its shadow. These skyscrapers, denying us our vitamins! But hey, smile, it's one Money-day morning for sure, and what do hustlers do on Money-days? They hustle, of course.

Matome, after washing, will always open the tap and wake me up – it will be my turn to wash. Then I will wake Molamo up and the line continues until we are ready to face the day clean. No breakfast here.

Today Molamo is having a very bad Money-day morning. He comes back to 207 early and says, "Give me three years and I will be thirty-three, and then I'm going to do something really ridiculous."

"What?"

"I don't know yet, but it will be something that this fucking stormy rainbow nation will notice and never forget, ever."

He has tears in his eyes, which are now drip-dropping out.

The Zulu-boy says, "They have lots of space in C-Max, enjoy it."

"They can't punish me," Molamo urges.

"Yes, they will just lock you up," I tell him, looking at him, knowing that he is being buried under an avalanche of uneasy, heavy feelings.

"I'm already punished."

"Who punished you?" I look at him, not even expecting him to give me a straight answer.

"I was born black. There's no punishment more painful than being born black."

"I noticed long ago that you're black, but my question is: Who punished you?"

"God has."

"Why is God punishing you, Molamo?"

"We have been, as black people, suffering for as long as there has been history. Everything bad happens to black people and even if I was a billionaire, living the life of a king, with slaves and servants, there would always be something which would remind me that I'm black and I don't belong."

"Molamo, I asked you why God is punishing you. What is he punishing you for?"

But this time his great mind fails him.

"You don't understand what I'm trying to tell you because you have become white yourself."

"No. I don't understand because there is nothing intelligent in what you are saying. Stop blaming God for what happened to black people, because, if anything happened, God made black people."

Then his voice changes, and this is not the Molamo that I know, the one that can answer any question, and the voice inside me wishes that Tebogo was here to witness with her own eyes what I'm seeing.

"You're thinking like Mandela caught in a web of lies and imposed pride, made by some international chequebook politicians in the name of democracy, which was just a good way to keep the masses forever suffering."

"Molamo, why are you talking about Mandela? We were talking about God punishing you."

"He was the first president, and he led this nation into a world of lies."

The dam bursts open.

144

"What he did was black betrayal, he betrayed us as a nation, all because of money. As I'm talking to you he's being honoured everywhere and respected by white people and their institutions the world over for betraying us. There's no way that you can sit at a table and smile, laugh and eat with the people that didn't see you as human a moment ago, and oppressed you, and then, seeing their back teeth, think that they suddenly see you as human."

The Zulu-boy once said to Molamo, "You're too sensitive, stop trying to read people and start believing what they are saying to you. Forget trying to see what is between the lines. Be like my brother here (he was referring to D'nice): read to know and for the joy of reading, okay? People will always window-dress and power will always be abused. Stop feeling betrayed by what somebody didn't do. They did what was fine for themselves at the end of the day. If you too were to hold a public office you would abuse it. I know I would."

That voice in me says: *You can't read lies and enjoy them.* But then what do you say when someone opens up and you see the pain that they are living under? I had to go because as he, Molamo, always says, "Give the man the stage and he'll get tired. He'll take his set, extras and himself off the stage without any fuss when the time is right."

I do as I'm advised and exit 207 because I have lived with him for too long and I know that if he gets in this mood it won't end today. I thought I could handle it but the world's ways and the world's history will make your heart heavy, make you think things that can make you hate your own blackness. Sorry to say it, but we are as black as . . .

*   *   *

I have an appointment at ten with David this morning to talk about film scripts, somewhere in an office park in Woodmead.

"If you are coming from the city take the N1 north, turn off at the Woodmead off-ramp, turn left at the first intersection, turn left again and left again, drive down until you find a big office block called the Woodmead Estate," he was giving me the directions to his office a day before.

David was my Business of Film lecturer before I . . . He is like Matome: he will always raise your hopes higher than high and eliminate any limits that you have set for yourself. For him the limit was the world.

Took a taxi to Alex.

The truth: I asked for a lift to Alex. The trick: you stand at the side of Louis Botha Road and only stop the empty taxis, then you plead your poverty; one is bound to give you a lift and, as always, one did. He drops me in Wynberg and from there I have to walk past Marlboro Drive to the Woodmead off-ramp and continue walking as directed. It's nothing. I usually walk from Hillbrow to Auckland Park and back to Hillbrow with ease. I give myself an excuse to walk, telling myself that I'm giving myself time alone to think, which works every time if I find it difficult when I'm busy writing – I just take a very long walk.

Got there.

My business: I have three scripts that I think are of international standard and I don't know what to do with them. Put them on the table and he takes the first one. He takes about forty minutes scanning the script, smiling to himself, but not saying anything. The silence makes me uncomfortable somehow, but I don't like to say anything. The second one and the third both shared an hour. Then he looks at me, smiling in disbelief.

"You wrote all this?"

He confirms his disbelief in me, but I have learned not to mind.

"Yes."

"Wow! You really wrote this? This is good. Do you know how many people write nothing but pure shit?"

"That's the reason I'm here."

"But I don't know how to help you."

Then, just as quickly, he rephrases that statement into a question. Then he considers it as a question, yes, because it doesn't sound like it has a question mark at the end and why rephrase it, if it was a question, and not wait for the answer?

"How do you want me to help you? Because there's nothing much I can do. What you have here is world-class material. I like the first one very much. I think that it would make money at the box office. It's . . . it's perfect, but I don't know. The industry is very complicated."

I give away a smile, trying hard not to show that it's a pain-filled smile, which I hope that he can't detect, but ten minutes later our business conversation comes to an end anyway.

"Well, good luck, my friend. If I hear anything I'll give you a call. I will talk to people. This one deserves to see reel life."

Then he takes out his wallet and out comes one of those things, a top-of-the-range one, which we all serve. Our business meeting becomes a pity conversation. I feel like I shouldn't take it. I don't want to take it, but if I don't it's going to create an impression of ungratefulness on my part. Sure, I need the money, I had to walk to this place, but this isn't business. This is exactly what Molamo was crying about this morning. Now, I'm feeling it too and I understand, but as Molamo always says, "It's Money-day, please don't miss it. You miss it, you've missed the whole week."

I remember after the free-to-air channel won the licence, our hopes were high again with the knowledge that we were going in the right direction. They invited companies and individuals to pitch whatever they had. The location: a luxurious hotel somewhere in Sandton. Our appointment: nine o'clock exactly. But we made it there long before nine because we had the feeling that always makes you lose control of yourself and over-smile.

Our turn came.

We got in and, after introducing ourselves and shaking hands, took the chairs without being invited to. The unknown Kopano (he is the big man there these days, very well-known) said, "You have three minutes to make us interested in your story."

Molamo jumped up like a soldier at war and said, "Say that again?"

"I said, you have three minutes to make us interested in your story."

"Is that how much time it takes you to write a single episode? How can we even interest you in a story when we don't know what you like and don't like? We are here to pitch a story, not to make you interested in one." He gave the surprised executive a copy of one of the stories that we were there to pitch. "If you're that good, read it in three minutes and tell me what the story is about. You have three minutes."

Silence fell until one of them managed to find words to say, "We are sorry."

"For what? Making fools of people? 'You have three minutes to make us interested in your story.' Well, mister, you have three minutes to read that story and tell me what the fuck it is all about. Do you have any fucking idea how much it takes to put an episode together?"

"Molamo."

"You motherfuckers think we are here doing three minutes of fame."

"Molamo, let's go."

And that was how we introduced ourselves. He scared them, because basically I think that they didn't have enough experience. With that

Molamo double-crossed our path with the free-to-air broadcaster. He looked at them and they saw the anger that said, "Say something and I'll step on you."

* * *

Got back to that damp, crumbling building. Who cares if it's damp and crumbling because in it, it houses a haven, our haven, 207. I pass the security checkpoint without saying a word to them. By now, Molamo had dusted himself down, put his face in some water and cleared himself off the stage after his own performance. I switch on the stove to boil some water for coffee, but then Molamo's pride searches him out and before you know it we are having some good chicken for lunch and not coffee but a very cold soft drink.

He calls Tebogo, "Can you come here now?"

"Now?"

"You heard me right."

"What's wrong now?"

"Oh! For me to see you there must be something wrong first."

If she was busy, believe me, for Molamo it can wait – family comes first. In less than two hours she'll be walking through the crumbling gates of our fortress and that voice in me asks: *Why is this crumbling? And then it answers itself: A former master can't serve a former slave.*

The old door to 207 will be open, waiting for her, and I know, she knows, why she is being summoned. Then I make way.

They look at each without saying a word, as if they are exchanging vital information about each other or just having impure thoughts about each other, and then I'm out of 207 and they . . .

* * *

Back to our haven, it is after eight and I find Modishi busy washing the plates, whistling tunes that can only be Modishi's. Molamo is busy with his own things – he's doing the cooking today. I look at them and don't say a word, then I turn and look in the mirror, trying to spot what the memories of today have done to my face and, sure, I don't like what the mirror reflects.

"Tebogo was here," says Modishi.

"Was she? When?" Molamo asks.

"She was here."

Modishi is a man who can detect someone based on how they smell and, true, Tebogo was in the haven.

"And, the last time, you said that you didn't want her any more. Why can't you just let the girl go? You don't want her and even if you do marry her you won't be happy."

Molamo looked at him. This guy!

I'll tell you the biggest secret of our haven. D'nice fiddled with Modishi's Lerato here in this very haven, on this double bed that Modishi and Lerato have been sharing since . . . not once, not twice, but three times, and they could do it again, just that D'nice doesn't want to any more. I sometimes even think that the abortions were not Modishi's seeds after all. This is between me, you, D'nice and Lerato; it doesn't go any further than it has, please.

And here is Modishi telling Molamo about relationships and happiness.

Molamo asks him, "Is it your business what I do with Tebogo or to Tebogo?"

"It just makes me sad and I don't think that you are treating her in the right way. You are taking advantage of her, abusing the love that she has for you."

"Modishi, I said: Is it your business what I do to and with Tebogo?"

"Your relationship with Tebogo is completely not my business, right, but it hurts sometimes to think about it, to see what you are doing."

Molamo shuts up, not willing to say anything else to this brother, and a voice in me tells him: *Your world and his world are not exactly the same.*

"Sorry, I just had to say that and get it off my chest."

Molamo forces out some laughter, "John the Baptist. It is not your business what I do with Tebogo, as it is not my business what goes on between you and Lerato, because, if it was, Lerato wouldn't be in your life any more because she doesn't deserve to even hold your hand, but it remains not my business, excuse the cliché."

Choose-day

Choose-day comes.

Matome has, as you know, an office in the city centre. This is a true African way of doing business under the African skies on African soil, where you get everything under one roof. As long as you have rands, Matome can do anything for you. The world can world you and he can turn the tables so you can world this big world, but at a price, which, he will tell you, is a budget price.

You know he is the owner/manager of a recording company cum printing house cum artist management agency cum everything. Sony doesn't even have as many employees as he has. There are journalists, lawyers, film makers and . . . They are all here on a favours-only/no-payment basis. That's Matome. Everybody coming in wants to talk to Matome.

The most unusual thing about Matome is that he always makes smiling-happy enemies in business.

"On your way up you'll have to step on other people's heads."

He made that statement after one of his customers stormed in, raging like a castrated elephant bull, but walked out like one of the female species after a session with D'nice.

"You can't go up unless you step on the heads of others. Not that I love it, but then how else does one go up?"

The first thing you would think when you walk in here is that it's only an office, but in truth it is a whole studio.

This is what happened.

These computers are brand-new; they came in unopened boxes, courtesy of not having strangers but friends in this world. He didn't buy them but gave the friend R800 as a thank you, and, if he hadn't insisted, the friend wouldn't have taken it.

This dear friend of Matome's came to the office once, only to find that this other computer, old and tired as it was, was giving us problems. He looked at the outdated thing and said, "Matome bra, you don't deserve to be using this old thing in a big office like this, no."

"I'm using it and it is working fine, baba."

"Bra. Before this week ends, you will have a state-of-the-art computer to work your magic."

"And where am I going to get the money from?"

"Believe. You are in Johannesburg and not everything has to be paid for. I know you're not working."

True to himself, the next day there was one delivered with a memory big enough for everything Matome needed to do, and the monitor was big, top end.

"You need anything, give me a call and maybe, maybe I can get it for you."

"I thank you."

Then the good friend brought this one as well, still in its box, saying, "Matome bra, you can use this one too. If I need it I'll give you three months' notice before I come pick it up."

The notice never came.

There are no soundproof walls here, but it is a recording studio and, unlike all the other music studios in this great city, where to record you have to pay a certain amount per hour, here you can record for free. And you are thinking: no. True, here you can record for free. There are studios in this city where they go for up to a month without recording even one track and that's not business, according to Matome. Here, there is always a queue of artists coming to record. But there's a catch, of course, where he takes advantage of people.

"You record people for free?" I asked him when he first started.

"I do, yes."

"And how are you going to get paid?"

"Somewhere along the line I'll make enough to survive. You see, you can't just record, there's a minimum number of cassettes and CDs that have to be produced, distributed and marketed. You can't just record and end it there."

Matome. He knows how to survive in Johannesburg.

Once, somebody introduced him to the PR manager of one of the big companies of our soil, knowing that this big brother could help the young brother. Matome said afterwards that he must have been more than fifty, divorced, with a nuisance of a son and a high-class whore for a daughter somewhere in the Johannesburg suburbia.

They got there.

Matome was with his clone, Wada, presenting their business. After talking over what they wanted, the big brother asked, "Whose company is Brains?"

Brains is the parent company of Brains Records, Brains Management, Brains Books and the many others that were not, as yet, active.

"It is mine."

Note that now the big brother is thinking that this little boy, who looks like he is no more than twenty-three, has a parent company that owns a record company. Then he goes way out of line.

"What kind of car do you drive?"

There was a pause as the young brothers, surprised by the question, wondered what to say, and for one second they wished that Molamo had been there because he would have reacted necessarily. Then Matome said, "No, I don't have a car."

But what can you say? You don't have a car. You don't have one, so why lie? You'll get a car someday, if you want to have a car. And, with that, the big brother rejected the small brothers.

They got back to their office to find that Molamo was still using their computer, and Matome said, "Some people are designed to hold others down; they are window-dressing, saying they are there to help."

"I knew you wouldn't get that one," Molamo said knowingly. He too had passed by the same office three times and was rejected every time by the very same big brother. And, being Molamo, he had to have a reason why and he knew why, and said, "Well, wake up, there is a Xhosa Nostra here. To have anything from government you must be Xhosa."

Wada asked him, "Molamo, what do you want us to do? Go toyi-toyi?"

"We will rise, I will rise somehow, look."

That was Matome, promising. He believed in himself.

Matome's office in the city centre. This is where I spend most of my days and nights, if I'm not Johannesburging. I'm here, Matome's here and, as you also already know, Wada is here day and night.

D'nice will be somewhere in the suburbs' digital studios; here there is real money and he's getting paid, and respected too, for his dexterous ways. He could be conducting a philharmonic orchestra with more than seventy people in it playing classical music, he could be conducting an adult choir somewhere in this Johannesburg, or putting together a rock album. You just never know with D'nice.

Modishi will be somewhere in the downtown studios doing what he likes to do the most.

Molamo is always busy with his writing, coming up with ideas, or at some meeting with potential investors for a film or a documentary.

And the Zulu-boy?

I never really know where the Zulu-boy is Johannesburging about, except that he is somewhere in the many music studios and wannabe music studios of this great city, pleasuring some musical instruments.

A sad tale

The week is gone, Wednesday is here and that's going too.

Let's take a midday walk around. Let us take a walk to . . . Well, we'll see where we end up. Lock the door. Pass the dead lifts on your left. Left into the stairs – they are clean and smell good. Down to the first floor, pass the dead lifts again, then left into the stairs. Out of the stairs, left, push the security door, and you are at the security checkpoint, which used to be a reception area.

"Hello, people, how are you doing today? Hope you all are doing very fine, I'm doing very well, myself."

Pass through this once grand entrance. It used to be the only door here when apartheid was the greatest security guard to all white people, but not any more. Democracy is here with its security gates, iron bars and security guards. Pass through another security door, not fashionable this one, but built for function.

Smell the contaminated Hillbrow air. Refreshing, or is it that I have learned to extract some leftover freshness from it?

Who cares? Or maybe you do? I hope you do.

You are in Van der Merwe Street, walk to your right, cross Claim, cross Quarts, Twist, King George and a left turn into Klein. Please notice and observe. Pass Pretoria, Kotze and Esselen, then turn right, keep walking, notice, see and observe with me here, jump a street into Captain. Notice this building on your right, the Hillbrow Theatre.

What about it?

Look at it very carefully and observe.

Looks dirty?

Didn't say that you should comment.

Pause.

Thank you.

Turn right into Twist, walk with me here. Relax, you aren't in any kind of danger. Walk like a true Hillbrowean. Walk it like it belongs to you, because, me and you, we have inherited this. It's ours now. Pass one street, pass another, and then make a left turn into Wolmarans.

Need anything to drink?

Yes?

No?

We'll buy something later, this is not the only twenty-four-hour supermarket around here, there's another one in Highpoint.

Need some quick midday relief?

No? You don't do that?

Good, maybe you'll get to heaven, but I tell you we are in hell now. Who cares if it's from one hell to another? At least we should enjoy this hell the best way we can.

Cross the street and turn right. I like this street but I don't know its name and I don't care what it is called.

The trees?

I don't know what are they called either, but I just like it when I walk in this street, though I think your nose noticed that it smells of urine.

You're now looking at the Windybrow Arts Centre. It used to be called the Windybrow Theatre but . . . it's a sad story too.

I need a banana, what about you?

No, or you just don't eat anything from street vendors?

Well, don't feel guilty, I know and I understand.

Keep going straight. Look who we are running into. This is Moloko, he's another sad story – a dropout of high school. He's here in the city terrorising city people and keeping the police working overtime. One thing I'm sure about is that I am going to pay him just for running into him. He's going to make me pay.

"Moloko."

"It's a good thing to run into you, to see a young brother from my home in this wild city." He kneels down, holding his hands together and performing a ritual of respect and honour. "It's a good thing to see, with my eyes, one from my home. One who understands and knows me not as the city people know me."

"How are you?"

"How do I look to you?"

"Looks to me like you are surviving very well."

"You are right, I'm surviving. I'm still here, isn't it? But I could do better if brothers like you, brothers from my home, cared enough."

"I care about you."

"I'm hungry and you don't even know that and you still claim you care, and, if I ask you for some money, you wouldn't even give me five rands for a loaf of bread, yet you say you care about this brother from your home in this wild city. Your care is like that of God. Well, how are you doing, my god? Good to run into you finally."

His eyes are running all over the place, he's checking his position and his friends' positions. This means we are disturbing a mission, an ambush in progress, someone is just about to be a victim of Hillbrow terrorism. I just hope, he or she, they don't die.

"I'm surviving, as you see."

I take out the first of Tito's bills and give it to him, feeling sad and sorry; that was to go in the collection for our haven tonight – I was going to demand a soft drink.

"You are doing more than fine to me, as far as I can see. Where is that beautiful woman of yours?"

"I don't know. She's no longer mine now."

"You let her go? You really let your woman go? This is unbelievable. The woman had reached Moshate, the land of bacon and eggs, the land of fast food and fast, easy life, formality and manners, three-course meals and table manners, four-by-fours for driving on tarred city roads, sports cars and holidays in five-star hotels. She had reached a land far better than the land of milk and honey, and you just let her go, like that?"

"She's the one who packed up and left me."

"No way, she would never do that to you. I don't believe you, you willingly let her leave. You pushed her to leave you."

"She left by herself."

"Told you that you should spat her."

I look at him, not willing to answer that, and he gives himself an answer. We shake hands once more.

Did you see that? The man didn't even say thank you. They are darkie brothers and they can do that, make you pay every time you talk to them. Moloko was the man back in high school. He could play with any woman he wanted back then, but now he knows that they'll wear you out. He used to be what all women wanted but look at him now. They have worn him down into a Hillbrow terrorist.

This place used to be a very nice little park.

See that building? That's Ponte. It's the building that Molamo's going to take a free fall from if he ever contracts Aids and, at the rate that he's going, that will be very soon. Just wait for it, you're going to read all about it in the daily papers.

Do you know a funny thing? I don't know what all these small streets are called, and, now I think about it, I don't really care as long as I know my way around because, basically, I'm not here to learn the names of the streets.

Keep going up, jump this one and turn left.

You see the second building? I used to have a girl who stayed there. She was one of those people who just came here because, for her, it was a trend, a fashionable statement. After much poking of her pokiness, I asked her a question: "What do you want with your life?"

"I don't know."

And that was a big turn-off, she just made me lose all interest in her and I never went back. She was going to some college in the city studying something-something travel and tourism. She matriculated, had a three digit IQ and could have been anything she wanted.

Forget her now, I used her and she abused me, but I can't help thinking that she is a sad story too.

This here is Hotel Lagos. That's what Matome calls it. The Sands Hotel. It's Lagos in the heart of Johannesburg. In Nigeria, corruption is what they all make a living from, and they are here too with their corrupt ways. Hotel Lagos, Hillbrow. Every time you come here, they are bound to ask you only one question: "Any business, any business?"

They don't even greet you, these black brothers.

It used to be my public phone, this place. I'd come here with Matome to make calls. It was Matome who showed it to me. They had mobile phones and there was a queue. With one rand you could call for five minutes and, if you were lucky enough, a patrol car would put its nose into the street and the phone man would just take the phone from your ear and disappear up the stairs into the Sands Hotel, sorry, Hotel Lagos, and you wouldn't have to pay for that call.

There was a time like now, when I found myself here, Hotel Lagos, and one of these African brothers said, "Me, I can do, get you anything as long as you have the money to pay."

Then I extended my hand and we shook, a very tight grip.

"Can you get me a broadcast-standard camera?"

"That I can get for you, ma friend, as long as you are paying?"

"Do you think I don't want to pay?"

"No, my friend."

"I'm not your friend."

"Please, please. You just wait here and don't get mad, African brother from another mother."

"I'm not your brother."

I looked at him as he disappeared into Hotel Lagos, well, the Sands Hotel. I was left in the company of his friends and they were all talking Ibo. I think they were talking Ibo or Yoruba. Ah! Who cares? They were talking African and I was obviously the topic of discussion.

I was being watched. They were trying to figure me out. What am I? I took out my phone and called Molamo. After waiting for five minutes I decided to go.

"My friend, don't leave, he is coming back soon."

"I don't have the time."

I picked up a piece of paper and wrote my number on it.

"Tell him to call me."

I said it like I own Hillbrow and, of course, I do own it. These Nigerian brothers are only here to help further corrupt the rainbow nation, they can get you anything as long as you pay.

Stop.

Take off your cap. A moment of silence . . .

Here, as you can see, a darkie brother bled to his death.

You don't want to look?

It is not from long ago, it must have been this morning.

Maybe he survived?

No, he didn't survive; look how big this pool is.

Let's hope he survived?

No. He's dead. He is dead and hoping doesn't change the facts here.

I don't know if there's someone who's supposed to come after the paramedics and clean up but it seems that, here in Hillbrow anyway, the rain is the only thing that cleans up after black brothers bleed to their death on the street. Sad. To the one that didn't survive Hillbrow. A moment of silence.

Let's keep walking.

Hand brake turn, walk faster.

I don't want to talk to that guy coming up the street and I hope he didn't see me. Now he is calling me. That was because of you. Shit! He's one of those people that I didn't want to meet.

"Sello."

I give him a hug. He's one of my cousins and he's here in the city doing the best he can in the corporate world.

"How are you doing?"

Well, he is doing very well in financial terms. He has a degree in something-something engineering from TWR and he's living somewhere in the suburbs, living the life of kings – a queen and a washerwoman somewhere in the background.

"You don't call any more."

"Finance is low."

"I met your woman a week ago. You're very lucky with that one."

"I wish I could see it that way."

You see, this is why I didn't want to talk to this guy, and, of course, he detects immediately that I don't want to talk about my fiancée.

"Are you sure that everything's fine with you? I was home last weekend and they say that you are not coming home any more."

I knew that was going to come up.

"They said that the last time they saw you was four years ago."

A voice in me asks him: *When did you last see me? You were going home, you could have called, I could have sent a message with you.*

"I'm going home tomorrow," I lied. I'm not going home, not now, not soon. "I'm taking a bus out tomorrow morning."

"Did you know that I bought a new car?" he asks, but he knows that I don't know, and he presses the remote control so that it acknowledges our introduction.

"This one."

"What happen to the Ie-Japan?"

"It was old, now I'm running with the times."

Well, if there is one thing on this God's green earth that impresses me it's a beautiful woman, of course you knew that, but second and last is a car that can handle from zero to hundred in under seven seconds. Who cares if speed kills? We're all going to die anyway. So, now, my heart is suffocating, jealousy mounts and turns into anger. I'm getting hot and can't handle it.

"It is a beautiful car."

Trying very hard to suppress these feelings and mean what I'm saying.

"Beautiful is not the right word here, brother, it is magnificent. Let me take you for a ride and, maybe then, you'll grasp what I'm trying to tell you here."

It's tempting but I know I can't handle it. I pass.

"No, some other time, we're doing some very important research."

"I'll drop by. By the way, what's your room number again?"

He forgot, good, thank you.

"I'm not staying there any more, I moved to Berea. I will call you."

"The week after next, I'm going home. I'm getting married, so you must come with me."

Then we shake hands and hug.

"Sure, I'll call you."

Why did I lie to him?

That's none of your business. Yes, he's my cousin but I didn't want to talk to him. Can you understand that and accept it?

Thank you.

Don't forget what I said?

Good, notice and observe. Let's go back to the corner of Van der Merwe and Claim in whichever way you think best. I have to buy some bananas from the vendor there. I don't know if all vendors are like him. This brother is Venda and, as you will see, as black as they come.

Oh! You noticed him? Yes, I did wave at him. You're really observing now. I like you, I can live with you. He's pure black and tall, strong too. I call him the magician, he sells everything illegal to those of us who find pleasure in losing our mind and looking at this world from another obscure angle. He doesn't just sell fruits, you can even get coke if you want it, or pilisi, for those who understand what that is. The funny thing is that I know that he's Venda and he's a vendor and I can talk to him anytime, but I'm sure I don't know him at all and, what's more, I don't want to know anything about him. To me he is only a businessman, as to him I'm only a customer, and that is all, that's our relationship.

"Vho vuwa hani?"

That's Venda for "How are you?"

"Ri hone."

I look at him, thinking that I don't have any idea about him and yet he knows the comings and goings of most of the people who stay around here.

He shakes the box of matches in his right hand and says, "You don't have any cash?"

It is a statement or a question, but I can't tell which.

"Why do you say that?"

He takes out a match and lights a cigarette, taking one long puff, and looks at me.

"Why do you look at me like you don't have any money?"

"There's a way that I look at you that means I don't have any money?" I take out a rand. "I need a banana."

He takes some bananas, putting them in a plastic bag and, as I hand him the rand, drops in the box of matches.

"Enjoy the bananas as well."

Then I know what's in the box, but I didn't notice when he swapped the box with the matches in with the one that he just dropped into the plastic bag. Where did it come from and where is the matchbox with the matches in? This is the reason I call him the magician. Then I smile and walk away without having to say a word more.

What colour paint is that on my block? I always thought it was cream.

It is?

Old cream, that's obvious. This is my home, has been my home for a long, long time. I just hope we don't find that tall security guard, he has a problem with me – he just hates me for merely being me. Which is natural, I understand, but I don't like it. He never says anything to Matome, but always has something to say to me.

Do you know that every time I come past here I ask myself how old this tree is?

This is where we left from earlier, this is where I stay, my block, notice and observe it. Someday I'm not going to miss this place, period. I'll be happy to move far away from it and, when I have moved far away I will never visit, even to pay homage, because there'll be no reason to do that.

Why am I staying in it then?

I don't have a choice, I don't have a choice and if I had . . . Well, we'll never know, will we?

He is here.

"Heita."

"Heita. Hey, come here."

I told you that he would have something to say to me.

"Didn't I tell you that you can't sleep with six of you in that single room?"

"Yes. You told me."

"So, what do you want me to do? You people are always troublesome, a week doesn't go by without us having to solve something because of you."

"Sorry."

"You are always sorry."

"Sorry and it won't happen again."

I'm used to him, he likes to irritate my ears every time he sees them, but I know how to treat him. I just make him think that he is almighty-powerful and has the upper hand. Then I walk to my room, knowing that if it comes to it I can do it again, that I'm going to do it again and there's nothing he can do about it. We are paying to be here and he is working because we are paying to be here.

This place is shining on the outside. The cleaners have been very busy. It makes me remember back home; there they had a habit of cleaning when they were expecting visitors, which I found very boring as I would have to clean the windows and wash my blankets just because somebody might visit. I didn't mind the cleaning, but why not do it for ourselves, rather than for others? But it's the same here. It's very clean all week, but look carefully and you won't believe your eyes, especially at the back, it's . . .

Well, I'm just here to be safe and I feel safe so there's no use in complaining. It's a black thing; we don't like to complain much, even if we have reason to. I like to say that we are a stream: block the stream, we will find a way around without complaining.

Once again, welcome to 207, I hope you are feeling our hospitality. You can have a banana or make some coffee. I'm going upstairs to get the angels of the night. We are going to sit here together, roll a smoke, puff and be happy for a couple of minutes – all courtesy of me knowing how to survive in Johannesburg.

You don't smoke?

Too bad, but hang around and maybe you can have it for free.

You don't do that either?

Wow! You mean you never ever? Never? Why not do it today? There's always a first time for everything.

No? You will never, either?

Jesus! Are you of this earth? You are lying to yourself, I can tell you that. Well, anyway, when you die you will go to heaven and, if not, then at least you'll die very healthy, but hang around anyway, you're going to tell me what you have seen, noticed and observed about me and this place. I'm coming right back.

I'm back and I'm sorry, but they are too tired to come have a puff with us. They have been working overtime lately. I forgot that it's month end and the mense have enough of the Titos.

So what did you see?

People living?

Yes, people are living out there. Is that all?

People living in rotting streets and buildings. That is a good one! And what have you observed?

Your observation is that you can't tell if they are happy or just pretending to be happy.

You have a question, ask.

Am I happy or pretending to be happy?

How can I answer that? You see, you have to enjoy what you are, be you poor or be you rich. I have to look at a very bad day, appreciate that it's a bad day, and try to find that which it has to offer me, then I have to learn to enjoy it. Then, if a better day comes, I can smile and be very happy, but if it doesn't come I'm still as happy with what I have. That's the motto that I live by; a belief, if you like. You can call it what you want.

Can I give you a very short answer?

Yes, I'm happy and I'm not happy.

What do I mean?

I have learned to be happy in all situations. This is a place where, when one sees his cousin he doesn't want to talk to him, but would rather run from him, and another brother makes you his bank in the dirty streets. It's all one big sad story and so I have learned to be happy in all situations.

Let me just puff and stop complaining. Let me just live it and forget about it, because there is nothing I can do about it and there is nothing you can do about it either. Or do you think that there is something that you can do?

I didn't think so.

Supper

Thursday: nine thirty-six or twenty-one thirty-six. The refugees are all in the safe haven.

"Ah! People, there is nothing to eat here," Matome commands, in that way of his. "I'm hungry."

This time he is speaking for us all.

He puts down seven rands. He's willing to spend seven rands. Molamo has ten rands but needs five rands back for some other business, tomorrow. Modishi drops in a ten and the Zulu-boy puts in a ten. D'nice gives ten rands and I put in sixteen rands, which is yesterday's change, and demand a two-litre bottle of soft drink.

I'm reading a Zimbabwean book, *The House of Hunger*; I'm not getting it and funnily enough I'm living in a house of hunger. The Zulu-boy and Modishi are going late-night shopping later, and I have to wash the dishes as D'nice will be cooking tonight.

At times like these I can't help but remember those bygone days, our first year in this city, when we had it easy. Matome would just walk into a supermarket and take whatever we needed and just walk out.

"Matome, remember when you would just walk into a supermarket and take whatever we needed?"

"No! I have forgotten about it, baba, forget it too, that was a long time ago."

He doesn't like me to remember, but life was simple then. This Matome and that Matome are very different. He no longer does that, but he still doesn't have the money to pay.

Why did he do it then and won't do it now?

He was eighteen years old then and eighteen is another time. He's twenty-seven now. If you're not mathematically inclined, that means that we have spent ten years together in this city.

I am cleaning the kitchen. The water is boiling and D'nice, as always, has to put some salt in the water to cook porridge. I don't know why he does that, but every time he cooks we have to have salted porridge.

Molamo starts talking now that the cooking has begun: "Matome, I saw Lerato today, she said 'hi!'"

"Tell her I say 'hi' too."

This isn't Modishi's Lerato. This one lives upstairs in 303 with her younger sister. Their beauty is worth dying for – Lerato is black and her sister is light and that is the only difference they have. This Lerato wanted to be Matome's Lerato and she was, for about three weeks, but then I fiddled with her and made her mine. Then I didn't like the way she thought.

Molamo asked him one day, "Matome, what is it with you and these women? You're not gay, but you're not straight either. Explain to me, please, because I can't figure you out."

"Baba, figure it out your way and you're right."

"Lucifer, I said I can't, or can't you hear well?"

"They are a waste of everything in life. They'll make you lose your direction and, by the time you wake up, your life is all a waste and they are still smiling."

Molamo looked at him, connecting together everything that he just said, and smiled. "What you are saying is that you fear women because they can waste your life."

"For me, the day that I have sex will be a statement that I want to be a father, and then I must father about five children."

"Well, good luck, satan, it's good to know that we have people like you around, people who know what sex is made for."

Life is funny, but you already know that. It was only then that I realised that Matome hates the female species and whatever it was that one of them did to him has impacted very badly. He can talk to them, charm them and even share a bed with them, but I have seen that, deep inside, he hates them.

Why does porridge have to have salt?

He said it tasted good with salt and so, every time he cooks, we have to eat salted porridge.

D'nice cooks like the genius he is, cooks porridge in less than ten minutes (but that's not including the time it takes for the water to boil).

"How's the script coming, Molamo?" I ask, just to kill the silence and give us a break from this house of hunger.

"These satans are holding me down as always, housing themselves inside a glass ceiling."

"They were born to hold you down. You scare them so they have to shut you outside," Matome reminds him.

Then the Zulu-boy and Modishi come back to 207.

Now, please count, it's now twenty-two eleven and at exactly twenty-two twenty-one we will start eating and Modishi, as always, will say a prayer over our food.

"Lord, God, the Almighty, we are here having our last meal of this great day; we thank You and ask that we should have some for tomorrow. Lord, You know us better than we know ourselves but we ask You, Lord, You who feeds us in the presence of our enemies, that You continue to do so for we are nothing without You."

Pause.

"Amen."

"Amen."

We don't talk when we are eating.

Then, at twenty-two thirty-two, Matome and I will be finished.

Like me, I guess when Matome was young he was fed the way that I was fed. Your mother would put you between her thighs. Someone would hold your hands and block your nose while your mother filled your mouth with soft porridge. You'd eat the whole bowl. It didn't matter whether you cried out or not. And it didn't matter whether you were full. They'd just block your nose and keep filling your mouth with porridge. And, after that, your little tummy would be so full that you'd just go straight to sleep. Well, that was some child abuse, I can tell you, but please don't say I eat too much – they made me this way.

Modishi is always the last one to finish, but tonight, we are having soft drink. If there's no soft drink there's coffee and, if that's not available, there's always a glass of water. We think we are living a choice-less existence but actually it's a very choice-full existence.

Now the kitchen is dirty again.

We would usually talk but tonight D'nice is hosting a girl and the Zulu-boy, as always, says, "D'nice, please do the job. Half-past twelve I will be coming back."

Then we give them the privacy of 207.

Pushing corruption

It's Friday. You are in Johannesburg. Your main reason for being here was, first, to go to that great institution of education and come out of it with a degree for a better tomorrow. This dream was not only for you, but for those that care for you and those that you have an obligation to and those you will have obligations to, but the institution unfortunately survives you.

Now. You have the keys to a flat and nobody to tell you how to conduct yourself or any kind of rulebook of self-conduct.

This is the funny part about this life of ours. We've got the Ten Commandments, the Constitution and manners. They can teach you how to have what they call 'good table manners' and they can teach you 'thou shall not commit adultery', but nobody ever explained anything about your feelings. Nobody ever said anything about love and loving people; everything I have learned about human relationships I have learned in the street, the hard way.

* * *

I go clubbing with Molamo. First, you have to look good, and by good I mean expensive. We have to put on labels, the latest things that are very expensive. Put on some expensive blue jeans, a black muscle top, a leather jacket and some top-of-the-range sports shoes – luxury that money can buy. Then some cologne, not too much, but a little, to draw the female species nearer. You shouldn't smell of it, you should smell like it's come from someone else, someone you have been close to. That

174

way even the high-class whores, who know everything, will ask, "What cologne are you wearing?"

Molamo always says that if they ask you, it's a triumph.

Then, when you are walking, you have to walk the part too. You have to walk, not like you own the world, but relax, walk like you don't want to walk. Imagine that walking to you is a strain, not because you are in pain, but because you are used to driving yourself around.

Clubs come and go, sometimes names and management change, but some things are always the same: we are here to war against Isando, to have a good time and maybe get a girl just to ice the night away.

The place: a nightclub somewhere-somewhere. The time: ten thirty. We are here early; if we had females with us I would say it's because it's free for them before half-eleven – our women have advantages all round – but the real reason is Boom Shaka. This particular Friday they're coming to perform here, to dance here and we have no reason to miss them.

We have already had a smoky holy war with Jah. Molamo doesn't like to roll it, instead he will empty a single cigarette, mix it with rum and maple and put it back in the cigarette, taking his time. You could even walk into a police station and have a smoke and no one would know.

"If Boom Shaka were performing and the ticket was equal to any of the visiting stars, I would pay," Molamo said, after being mesmerised by the girls.

I knew I would pay a thousand just to see Boom Shaka do their thing on stage. I know that there'll only be the four of them on stage – no dancers or special effects and no big screen. But hey! They'll do things to you, believe me, they will.

Molamo looks at the members of the female species that have already gathered in the club and says, "These are our friends; they, like us, don't have enough so they resort to freebies."

True, there are more females than males.

Molamo dances to the song that's playing, just to grab some attention. It's a statement. Look at me, look at me, I'm here now. And whoever notices, notices.

"Notice that girl over there."

The girl had a body put together the way our African women should be. A powerful body, promising three times more eroticism than Lebo of Boom Shaka and, let me tell you, she got our attention. African women are not queens – a queen means servants, slaves and guards. They are women with bodies as big as Africa that can bear all with a smile. Her dancing and the smiles she was giving away said: Don't treat me like a queen for I can't be a queen. I don't want a king but a man who is man enough.

"Ja! The one in black dancing with that boy," I answer.

"I have to kiss her butt today."

I look at him. He is the kind of brother who always has condoms in his pocket. He always says: "No soldier goes to war and returns without firing a bullet, that would be a disgrace to the battalion, and if I ever did I would be a disgrace to Molamo."

She's dancing, moving her elegant body elegantly, giving away a preview of better things, while the boyfriend is like that big black statue on Church Square, more like he's aroused.

We walk to the bar, feeling the attention we are getting, feeling like we are walking down the red carpet, surrounded by cheering fans and lit up by camera flashes, to receive the best film, best director, and best newcomer awards at some film festival.

I greet the barman, who noticed us when we were still metres away, and wait. Molamo puts his hand in his back pocket and out comes a roll of R200 notes. He looks at it and then puts it back and takes another roll from the left pocket, a roll of R100s, and then puts it back again, while I order our drinks from the now overwhelmed barman: "Prepare us a round of two tequila golds with salt, two Amarula blow jobs, vanilla ice cream topped with Kahlua, two Mexican assholes, two Bloody Marys, two springboks and two dumpies."

By now Molamo is finished with his show – in one of his front pockets there was a thick roll of R50 notes and, in the other, a thick roll of twenties and tens. I pat him on the shoulder.

"I'll pay. I'm paying today. Well, tonight."

I pull a R200 roll from my wallet and put a note on the table as we smile at each other knowingly.

"We got them good tonight."

The barman puts the beers in front of us and then one of each drink in a line in front of me and one in front of Molamo. We look into each other's eyes, challenging each other, then, in less than twenty-seven seconds, we are left with only the dumpies in our hands.

The barman is smiling, saying to himself: Shit, these guys! I'm not exactly sure whether he felt sorry for us or whether he had enjoyed the expensive show, but then he does what all barmen like to do: "So, first time I see you guys here?"

"So, you know everybody who comes to this joint?"

"Nearly all."

Without turning, Molamo directs the barman to the perfectly structured girl.

"Do you see that girl next to the stage dancing?"

"The one in black?"

"Yes. What's her name?"

"I just know her face. And that's her man, they are always here together."

"Every girl as beautiful as she is has a man."

"She's a regular. They come here all the time."

He gives us back our change, and I give him a nice tip, then Molamo takes a fifty and gives it to him.

"When she comes to get herself something to drink, give it to her for free and just mention that I said, 'Dance, please.'"

He agrees as I shake and turn my head. The Isandos are now doing their thing. I take the packet of cigarettes out of Molamo's pocket and light one, while Molamo says to the barman, "Even if the boyfriend is here with her, tell her that I said she must just lose herself and dance." Making sure that he knows exactly what to do.

I turn around and look at the young, grooving masses. They are waiting for something big to happen and, sure enough, we are all waiting. Then I spot some friends of mine, city-made from Botswana. They're here in the city chasing a dream but, now, they're here to harm time and boredom. They are fortunate to have their national budget backing them up and they can keep buying and buying till they need to be driven home. I will need them because after that very expensive show I have nothing.

You didn't get it?

You wouldn't. But don't worry, they didn't get it either. They all just got it the way we wanted them to get it because that was all the director wanted in the picture. The truth: we had about R600 and, after the entrance fee, the drinks and the tip, we are now left with just under R300 – and some of that hidden away where only the great god of Isando can retrieve it.

Those were not really R200 notes but some counterfeit ones and some look-feel-like money papers just to make the roll look thick. My fat wallet has nothing but useless things in it to make it look that fat. Like I said before, it was a show.

One night the show backfired.

It was well directed and achieved what it was intended to achieve. But that night our other friends noticed too. They were not going to let some cheese boys with that much money walk away, so they watched us. When Molamo got himself something to pad, he went to pad it in the parking lot and, just after putting on that preventing thing with his trousers down, they ambushed him, making away with R4 000 counterfeit and R260 real ones. Luckily they didn't take anything other than that.

These are my friends. We act like it's a big thing that we are meeting again like this. One of them is Eugene. I'm overwhelming him. We used to go to film school together; we used to be team players in all things back then, before I . . .

He holds me with his left hand, the right hand holding one of those from Isando, and says, "Hee! Monna wa reng? O sa tshela?" But he never really expects an answer, so I keep quiet.

When everything has died down I venture, "Can I buy you a round? Let's go have a round on me." And they look at me with some sort of amazement.

"Hee! Eer! Ga o na madi, e re rona re go rekele bojalwa, maSouth Africa ga a na madi. Ga o na madi."

Which, directly translated, is: "You don't have money, let us buy you beer, you South Africans don't have money. You don't have money."

True. I take no offence at that and they buy for me. I wasn't actually intending to buy them beer. No. You know my financial situation. It's just that it's not nice to ask people directly to buy you a round. I always let them volunteer to buy for me because it's true, we South Africans are poor people. There's no use getting mad when someone points it out.

Anyway, they are already drunk (you can tell because they forget to speak English and only speak their home language when they are drunk) and they won't miss the money. Then I know that even if the night was longer than usual I've got friends here who will make it unnoticeable.

Just before Boom Shaka take the stage Molamo's targeted beauty and her man go to the counter to buy some more beer and the barman gives them the beers without taking the money, saying, "He said that you must let yourself go and dance like tomorrow's not coming."

"Who was that?" the beauty asks.

"I can't see him now."

"He knows me?"

"No. He just said that you must let go and dance."

"Going to dance, sweetie, after Boom Shaka," she says, sticking her middle finger out and looking at her boyfriend. "Sweetie, pay, please."

He does as he's told, but she goes back soon after that to have the whole story, alone. "Can I have those beers, please?"

"I thought you didn't want them."

"Sweetie, you wouldn't like it if your girl took things from strangers, would you?"

"You're right, but they told me to tell you even if he was with you."

"Who?"

"Some rich boys, they came in here with style. Two very expensive guys. The one danced some moves before they had drinks, everybody noticed them. They were wearing jeans and white tekkies."

"Yes. They were wearing leather jackets."

"Ja!"

"Tell him I said thank you."

"So, what's your name, so that if he comes back I can –"

"Nandie. Pass the message. Say that I sealed it with a kiss."

It worked, it always works. Seeing is believing. After another visit to the barman I deliver the message, shouting in his ear, "The disciple of Isando says the girl's name is Nandie."

"I'm going to talk to him and get all the details."

By that he meant that he wanted to know about her body language. How she reacted to the news.

* * *

After Boom Shaka get off-stage the DJs are at work, it's a one-night stand. Molamo finds the place where she had been dancing and starts a circle there, doing what he does, and it becomes the biggest circle I've ever seen. I'm witnessing people moving and shaking dexterously and there is no doubt that somewhere in there somebody is aroused.

Nandie took the stage unwillingly, challenged by Molamo. As they dance he touches there and there, then, likewise, she touches there and there, and slowly they mend into one. Animal instincts of courtship, a conversation develops within the dance. Then the boyfriend separates them as Molamo was overindulging, and, as he does so, another one joins Molamo, and Molamo does his thing with her until her man has to rescue her as well. I tell you, Molamo can dance.

Molamo takes a bow and takes himself off the stage, and the dexterous takes over to prove that he's not the only one who can dance, as we all watch, clapping hands and shouting it out. I pat Molamo on the shoulder, he is sweating now, and shout, "Can I have a smoke?"

He gives me the whole pack and, by that, he means that he has had enough of this Jah thing, has had enough of keeping healthy. It is a culture and religion, it keeps you healthy. I even heard an allegation that the goat-bearded president is part of the holy war in his very private moments, and I believe it, look at the guy.

I buy a beer and sit at a table and puff, courtesy of Jah. I close my eyes, turning my head, feeling . . .

"Can I have a puff, please?"

I open one eye and look.

"Can I please have a puff? Please."

"Puff."

She wants to take it from my hand.

"No, no."

I look at my cigarette, then I look at her, then I take one very long puff and blow a smoke ring into her face and she turns her head in a circle trying to inhale it. I take another puff and, holding it in, I beckon to her and, for a moment, she hesitates, and then we kiss, exchanging the holy smoke.

"Where is your man?"

And she never had a chance to answer that.

"Have a beer."

"I don't drink that."

I put some money on the table.

"Go have yourself a beer of your choice."

"Don't want a beer, but a puff."

I take a puff and take a look at her, and then I start to think very impure things. I give her a smoky smile and she gives me another kiss . . . And, with that, she became the first of the DJ's phenomena, a one-night stand. It just happened.

I come back smiling freely and run into Molamo who was looking for me.

"Satan, where were you? I was looking all over, excuse the cliché, all over for you."

And he holds a used condom in my face and says, "You see? Smell it."

Putting it in my face.

"This is how she smells after all the deodorants and colognes. This is her God-given smell – as individual as her fingerprints."

Fate

Out

Have you ever lived with somebody for so long that you know what they'd do each and every morning when they'd wake up? Understand everything about them, know that late at night, just before they'd sleep, they would pick up a newspaper and look at it, not intending to read it, but just to look at it? Then they'd go to the toilet and come back, and say, "People, I'm sleeping."

That's friendship. That was my friendship with Matome.

He came back one night and announced that we were going to have the out-of-Hillbrow party.

"Ja!"

"When?"

"This coming Friday, baba."

Could you take that seriously? You should. You should never write people off. Things change, let me tell you that. Believe me. I know.

Friday came.

I was with a very beautiful member of the female species: Bridgetté. Bridgetté was a Soweto girl that I'd picked up at the library. She was a student, poet, writer, party animal, drug dealer, lesbian, socialite and an intellectual all rolled into one. She had an opinion about everything. I had forgotten about the out-of-Hillbrow party.

When we got to 207 there were enough of Isando's products filling it to drown the homeless of Johannesburg for a couple of months. Then I remembered that Matome had said that we were having a party.

Whoever was whoever was there; all the 207s and Matome's loyal slaves. I was the last one to make it. True enough, we were having an out-of-Hillbrow party, and the Zulu-boy, Molamo and D'nice were already drowning deep. Well, if you can't beat them, you join them. And I did just that.

Matome and Modishi were the only two not drinking. Modishi was the DJ of this out-of-Hillbrow party, playing music that our guests had never heard before. The idea that we were going to play our very own music had been in the original plan of the party.

You like it?

You don't like it?

Ah! Well, we are playing it anyway.

They loved the sound, wondered whose music it was, and that made it a very special occasion from the start. I can tell you that there were dreamers, gold-diggers and roughnecks, beggars and the homeless, players and pawns, et cetera et cetera.

No angels of the night tonight, sorry, the angels were all at 207. They stopped doing their business just for us, stopped to come and celebrate at our out-of-Hillbrow party.

That was Matome, he was that capable.

207 proved to be a very small place so we moved to the street, Van der Merwe Street, and then everyone just came, helping to dance Hillbrow out of our system. The police soon came as well and they shut off the music because the party was not authorised.

Believe me, please, when I say that Matome rose to every occasion. Matome shook hands with the police and had a talk with them. Then they apologised and the music was playing again. They left with a case of those intoxicating products from Isando.

With that I gave away a priceless smile. I just couldn't help myself. I was feeling like Sani Abacha swarmed over by white prostitutes somewhere in Switzerland. Except, of course, that the ones that were swarming over me were black and not all of them were prostitutes.

You don't understand?

Let me just shut up.

I was having a good time until Matome proposed a toast.

"Thank you all for coming."

I had never heard Matome talking like that, in that voice. It was not like his voice; it had changed, or maybe I was just lost to the war with Isando. He sounded like a billionaire at an occasion that he knew he had to come to, but in which there was no profit for him.

"When I came here I wanted to have a degree, but I failed because . . . Well, Noko wrote about it, he says it's a very sad black story. Things of our world work in ways that you wouldn't understand. So today is my graduation day because today I have a degree, not from any university, but from life; and with this, life's degree, I'm sure I have survived and I know that, sure enough, I will survive. Tonight, I have invited you all here to come and celebrate with me, this celebration that I had planned from the first day I came to this great city. It's not that I hate Hillbrow and it's not like I love Hillbrow, but a toast to this day, the day that I am moving out of Hillbrow for good . . ."

He continued talking on and on, but I couldn't hear him any more. This out-of-Hillbrow party was supposed to be our out-of-Hillbrow party and now, all of a sudden, it was Matome's out-of-Hillbrow party.

I looked at Molamo, then at Modishi, but, from that moment on, I can't tell you anything about the party. My mind just stopped at that point, with the words, "This was supposed to be *our* out-of-Hillbrow party" on my lips.

* * *

When I woke up I was in front of the door to 207 and on my left was Molamo, who was smiling, holding a dumpie in front of his face like he was checking the contents, checking how much was still left inside. He was finishing a story that he was telling me: ". . . that was going to be a very sad life. Think about it, I mean, that life was going to be very boring, excuse the cliché."

"Ja! You are right."

That was me. I had to respond.

I took a drink from a bottle of Isando that to my surprise was still three-quarters full. Between us were fourteen cold ones still waiting to do what they do best.

"Now you see it my way. You get it, satan."

"I see it your way."

"See it my way. I'm telling you the truth, it doesn't hurt or it hurts. I tell it like it is, excuse the cliché."

Even today I can't tell you what it was we were arguing about and I can't tell you what happened at the party. Can't tell you what happened to the beautiful Bridgetté, except for the fact that she called twenty minutes later asking how I was, and it was at that moment that I re-alised where my thinking had got stuck: "It's not that I hate Hillbrow and it's not like I love Hillbrow, but a toast to this day, the day that I am moving out of Hillbrow for good."

From that moment on there was so much rage in my blood that I couldn't stand up.

Why?

Because Matome was moving out of Hillbrow before me. I was not happy. Matome, that foolish boy, was moving on to higher places and leaving me, us, behind.

Can you feel my rage?

It was then that I understood why a black person would bewitch you for moving up in this life. It was then that I understood why a dear friend of mine lost his mind and died weeks after passing his matric with flying colours and winning a scholarship. Because there was a heart just like this one, that didn't like it, and that heart knew a way of stopping him and it did.

* * *

We were all there, still doing harm to what was left of Isando's best or they were finishing us off, one or the other, when Matome came back to 207 to say his goodbyes.

D'nice was dead-drunk-asleep with one for sleeping in his hand and his thumb blocking the mouth so that nothing could get in and nothing could get out. He looked like a very expensive collapsible chair that had collapsed.

"What do you think you are doing?" he asked Miss Lebogang, as she tried to take away the bottle.

"Give me the bottle."

"No. I'm still drinking." Then he curled himself into a foetal position, bent his legs until his knees were touching his chest, covered his face with his hands and, finally, said, "I'm not sleeping."

True, he wasn't sleeping, but I don't have a description for what he was doing.

The Zulu-boy was the only one still standing up. He looked like he was the only one who was winning this war.

"You can't drink with me," he said, declaring a victory for himself.

"And, lucifer, what do you think I'm still doing?" Molamo asked him.

He was lying flat on the floor with a bottle next to him.

Modishi was in the loving hands of Lerato. Lerato was in the protective hands of Modishi. She was dead drunk and he was sober as a lion. Modishi and Lerato.

"Modishi," she said with that graceful voice, "Modishi, I'm the luckiest girl, I am."

As the tears pushed themselves out he wiped them off.

"I am and I don't know why."

Matome left. "Ah! Nna ke a tsamaya, batho." His tone was not the one we were used to, and I couldn't say whether he felt sorry to be leaving for the last time.

"Ah! I'm going, people."

Inside I was really hurting, but I couldn't tell him that. Outside I was putting up this Chinese smile, but inside I was really hurting.

"Here is to Matome, have a great future, I just hope you get yourself a remarkable woman," I managed to say, raising a bottle of Isando's best and pouring out the beer onto the wooden floor. "May she be a woman with, and of, character."

"You will see. You will see," he said, the second time with even more promise.

Then the Zulu-boy poured beer onto the wooden floor, watching it disappearing slowly between the boards, into the dirt-full spaces, as if he suddenly regretted doing it, and said, "Here is to Matome, the Pedi boy."

"Then I'm going to have a few children."

"How many?"

"You will see."

Matome was the wife of 207, he was the one responsible for all that needed female intuition: paying the rent, buying the bags of rice and porridge and all the things that we needed. If one of us was cooking and something wasn't there, he would always know where it was or tell us if it was finished. Officially, this haven was rented under his name. We were just staying there.

"Let me walk you out. Let's walk Matome out, Zulu-boy."

We walked him out. We walked past the dead lifts and into the stairs. There the evidence of joyfulness was plain to see: empty cans, broken bottles, used condoms and vomit.

On the first floor we found the cleaning woman, who said, "Matome, you see how much dirt your friends have made."

"This is the last time you will ever have to clean up after me and I thank you very much."

"Thank you very much," I repeated after him.

And Matome hit the Zulu-boy to have his say.

"Thank you, mama."

Matome gave her one of Tito's business cards, the fourth one in the range that helps you to do your business easily. She wanted to say thank you but he stopped her: "You don't have to thank me."

And, as we were looking at the evidence of one of Hillbrow's greatest ever, I noticed some more used things that they say are for prevention of Aids. The Zulu-boy saw them too and commented, "Shit, some people were to be born nine months from yesterday if somebody hadn't invented condoms. That would be how many days from now?"

"Two hundred and seventy-five, plus or minus."

"Fuck, in two hundred and seventy-plus days human beings, lifelong tributes to when we were getting out of Hillbrow, were to be born."

"When Matome got out of Hillbrow, Zulu," I corrected him.

"Ja!"

Outside in the street the evidence was also plain to see. I looked at the tree and thought about its choice-less existence. It was waiting for one thing, waiting for the day that somebody at the municipal office declared it dangerous to the public, and then they would come and take it out of the ground and maybe plant another one.

I had run out of words and the bottle slipped from my hand, a thousand pieces followed. They looked at my stupidity without a comment.

"Matome."

I opened my arms and we hugged and the Zulu-boy, not liking what he saw, turned around and walked back, saying, "Matome, I always knew you were a fag."

Then Matome kissed me on the lips, a butterfly kiss.

"I always wished to have a brother till I met you."

He got into his car.

"You should have control, even a kiss from a man makes you lose yourself. Have self-control."

And that was it. After thirteen years and thirty-one days in this city together, that was it. Some people are never believable.

Matome

We left the two hundred and seventh haven. We moved out, one after the other; it was like we had somehow lost the rhythm. We had celebrated Hillbrow out of our system and, after the party, we hated Hillbrow. We couldn't stand it any more.

"Poverty and suffering unites people," Molamo said once when he was writing a book about a young man, Mokiditi, from rural South Africa, who went to school through the will of his uneducated parents and got a degree, but after that couldn't even stand to look at his own mother.

"Good living makes people greedy and greed divides them," Molamo concluded, as no one had anything to say after the first statement.

Greed and ambition, how different are the two? When does greed overcome ambition and where does one put jealousy in the picture? How does one measure oneself if not against friends? I believe that good living divides people. Look at TKZ, they once sang: "We love this place. Oh! We love. Oh! We loved it here. We love this place."

Then they went solo.

It never works. Poverty put them together and good living can't build on what poverty began. It can only destroy them because that which is raised in poverty can't be tolerated out of poverty.

Anyway, it was one hell of an out-of-Hillbrow party; we, he, made Hillbrow stand still. Don't know how many parties, wannabe and nearly parties are held on a Friday night in Hillbrow, but I can tell you that nearly everything else came to a halt because we, he, Matome, was having an out-of-Hillbrow party. The Hillbroweans didn't know that they were celebrating to extract Hillbrow out of us, out of him; they were just celebrating, and they left their parties and wannabe parties to celebrate with us.

Matome had said, long ago, when we were still planning this out-of-Hillbrow party, "You see, baba, the Israelites took forty years to reach the land of milk and honey. The reason being?"

"They didn't have cars and cargo jets, fool," the Zulu-boy told him.

"Yes, you might say that but in actual fact it was because they had to de-slave-ise their minds, they had to learn not to think like slaves. Remember, at one point, they thought slavery was good. So we will be partying in Hillbrow to de-Hillbrow-ise our minds because I don't like it here but, having to spend every day here, you learn to like it somehow, it just becomes your life. I won't want to miss anything Hillbrow because there is nothing to miss. Missing something about Hillbrow would be a step backwards into slavery."

"What? Satan, are you listening to what you are saying?"

"Zulu, can you stop live-loving Hillbrow for a moment and realise that not everybody likes it here as much as you?"

"That, Matome, is black betrayal."

"Molamo, please tell this Zulu boy what black betrayal is."

"Black betrayal is when a Xhosa fat cat tries to intellectualise our suffering and reason away our liberty. Worse still, black betrayal is when you can't criticise a government of Xhosa people, a government elected by black people for white people."

Molamo took that from a poem by Mbongeni Khumalo. I have nothing but great respect for that poet, he just tells it how it is, and Molamo only modified it a little bit.

"Zulu, that is black betrayal." Matome rested his case.

"Molamo, you support what this satan is saying?"

"Lucifer, wake up and smell the rot, excuse the cliché, but wake up anyway. We are all living and laughing at our own misery here. Don't blame Matome for the way he feels, it is his choice."

Matome said, "Zulu, I wasn't trying to be political with you, I believe that an injury to one is an injury to one. I'm not expecting anything from anybody but myself. And, when I get out of here, I will be doing it for myself. I'm saying it today, while I'm still here, that the day I get out of here I'm not coming back, even for a visit, because I hate everything here."

"Because you hate it here? Well, we, I, Molamo, understand you fully, Matome."

"Lalelani la," the Zulu-boy commands, "in that black book that's called a Bible there's a verse somewhere that says when you rejoice because you have had a good day remember that a bad day is coming too, because both days were made by the same person."

We all look at him in surprise: the Zulu-boy quoting from the Bible.

"If both days were made by the same person, why not enjoy them all the same?" We are still looking.

"What I'm saying is that if we are here, if we are living here, let's be really happy here and love it here so that if we ever achieve our hopes and dreams, we can sympathise with those left here, and if we don't make it out, we'll still love it here because it is all we have."

"Good point, baba, but how do you expect us to be happy and love it here when we have children living in the streets, sniffing glue? How do you want us to love it here? Should we just keep pretending that we can't see them?"

"Matome, don't cry."

"Because it's cold and inhuman living here."

"Cry, Matome, cry, but those street children have accepted the fact that they are what they are; when you look at them there are no tears in their eyes because they're happy being what they are. They have their hopes and dreams, but they are happy with what they are."

"It is not by choice."

"Matome, you're not here by choice either."

Matome looked at the Zulu-boy, holding back whatever it was that he was about to say because there was no use.

"The day is coming when I will be leaving and, when I get out of here, I won't be taking anything with me."

True to himself he didn't take anything but a pile of very important documents that he couldn't do without.

*　*　*

He bought a house in Victory Park, at a discounted cash price, and moved in the same day. He called me and told me that he wanted me there. He said that, in his heart, it was our out-of-Hillbrow party.

But the good red blood that my heart once used to pump was no more.

Why?

Jealousy. Yes. This uncontrollable black jealousy that I never knew I had in me, put a full stop to the longest non-blood relationship that I ever had.

You don't propose friendship to people. Only blood can do that – it's pure chemistry – then you wake up and you have a best friend. Matome was my best friend. I never thought that something like jealousy could end that.

Was I the only one jealous of DJ M. A. Tome baby?

No.

We all were.

The dropouts?

It hurt them, I can tell you, and you could see it in 207. We would talk and laugh together, but we weren't the same. There was always this part that was missing, that voice, that laugh.

"People, I'm sleeping. People, I'm eating. People, I'm taking a bath. People, I'm going."

We wanted to forget that there ever was such a voice, ever such a man, a character. We all wished that he would die.

Except for D'nice. He was happy. Matome made it and there were no second thoughts. He was happy for Matome.

* * *

He's living it up in Centurion now, the dropout cum . . . cum DJ M. A. Tome baby cum husband cum father. To Molamo, he is a cum back-stabber.

Why?

Guess.

They can't even look at each other in the eye any more. Matome double-crossed Molamo's path, or that's how Molamo sees it anyway.

He has a wife now and a baby girl who is about two and a half and his wife is pregnant again. Matome always said that he would need to have about seven mirror images.

He invited me a dozen times to come to his home, but I always found an excuse. He felt it once and said, "I feel that you are kind of distancing yourself. I'm still your friend. I feel like you are pushing me away."

Pause.

"You are more than a friend to me; we have been through too much together."

Pause.

Then I ask, "How's Basedi doing as a wife?"

"Come see her for yourself. You're my friend. I still need you."

And with sadness in his voice he cut the call.

* * *

I did visit once, out of curiosity more than anything else.

Matome married Basedi in a ceremony that was the end of Matome and Molamo. He didn't even show his face at the wedding. Molamo took and abused all of Matome's wannabe girlfriends, but when Matome took only one of his ex's they couldn't look at each other.

Been there.

It was heavy, like I was in the wrong place.

We were drinking some expensive brandy from an in-house bar. This house? The house was huge and looked like those houses in the magazines. Houses nobody deserves to live in. But here was Matome living in this one. I asked him, "What's Molamo missing, that he has to be so angry?"

"Molamo wanted Basedi just to fuck her, and I don't know what he's so angry about because he fucked her enough and then he let her go. I'm not fucking her. For me, she's a golden incubator and I hope it hatches golden chicks. I can't tell you what Molamo's so mad about."

After enjoying his brandy it was time for me to leave. I was going to Melville, so he drove me there in a sports car. Dropped me right in front of the gate, and then gave me an envelope.

I looked at him, not knowing how to say what I was about to say, not knowing how would he handle it and he looked back, expecting something.

"Do you know, Matome, I'm not happy for you. I'm very jealous and I wish often that you die. I was never happy for you since the party."

I could swear that the voice wasn't mine, but he didn't seem to notice. He just smiled and laughed an indulgently rich laugh, and said, "Baba. I know, I can see. That's because there's God in you, just as there is God in me, and if it was the other way around, I would be jealous of you. If God wasn't jealous, the world would be a different place. But do you know something? I'm not happy for you either, but, you know, not being happy for each other doesn't mean we aren't friends any more."

"You should not talk like you are in Hillbrow any more."

"That was a tribute to Hillbrow, baba."

We looked at each other for a moment, speechless, and then he drove away.

I knew what was in the envelope so I put it in my pocket and attended to my business there. But, later, when I opened the envelope I discovered that I was wrong. It wasn't some small change, as I thought, but a big cheque.

It sealed our separation. He never called me again and I never called him.

D'nice

D'nice was the second to bid farewell to 207. He just decided to move in with the beautiful Miss Lebogang, of course.

He de-havened the haven slowly. At a snail's pace. He would leave for three to five days at a time, come back, pick up some things and disappear again for a few days. Then he would come back to pick up this and that as well, until he officially broke the news: "My playtime is up."

Maybe he expected a big response, but he only got a glance from Molamo.

D'nice said it once again, this time very slowly, as if the time was really up. He opened the closet, looking at it as if he knew that he would miss looking at it, and said, "Time is up. Game over."

"What game?" the Zulu-boy asked.

Molamo asked too, "What game are you talking about?"

"Well, I'm thinking of moving in with Lebo."

"Do you want our approval or are you not sure about something?" the Zulu-boy asked him, while Molamo looked at him with a degree of disappointment.

"Parting is always such sweet sorrow, excuse the cliché," he said, mimicking Molamo. That was obviously what he had been expecting him to say.

Molamo smiled and said, "Lucifer, life as you know it here is sorrowful, but where you are going you know nothing about it; maybe it won't be worse than this."

"I am moving in with Lebo."

"Good luck, Tswana-boy."

"Lebo is eight weeks pregnant and I got my job back."

"Twice good luck to you, Tswana-boy. A man must work, a man must raise himself."

"If I hadn't got caught up in this music thing, I could have been rich by now."

"Is that disappointment or resentment? Because a moment ago you spoke like a real Zulu man," the Zulu-boy said, looking at him.

"Both, you could say, disappointment and resentment."

"We have been living a great life. What do you resent?"

The Zulu-boy gave him his hand, looked him deep in the eyes, and said, "You were in a system but you didn't live in the system. Yes, you are a sick bastard, you could have been better than you are."

"Jack of all trades is a very confused man," Molamo said to himself. And D'nice looked at him and responded, "A ghetto intellectual is a very unhappy man."

Molamo offered him his hand, "Welcome to fatherhood in advance. Nine months minus eight weeks in advance."

We shook hands for the last time.

"D'nice, it's been very good living with you, brother. Be a wonderful father and equally wonderful husband."

"Do my best."

"Wish you luck."

"Do I need it? Lucifer, I don't think I do. I don't need luck because I am going to play both parts very well, thank you."

Turned out that he needed it very much. I never knew D'nice to be a violent man, but he became violent. Miss Lebogang thought that he would change, but the only thing that changed was that he immersed himself deeper in Isando. She is having his second child very soon and the first one is only two years old.

They can't even stand to look at each other any more.

Modishi

Modishi is still madly in love with Lerato and, every now and then, I still wish to love and be loved like that.

He married Lerato.

Modishi and Lerato, they're still together because he gave her his heart with love, and, when he gave his heart, he chose not to see some things and forgave her for others.

"Thinking about it, honestly, I don't blame her for doing what she has done. She is still a child and it wasn't right of me to take advantage," he told the 207s after he'd recovered from having his seeds end in ash.

The Zulu-boy looked at him and said, "The Baptist, now you are the one who is sorry, or am I not hearing you right?"

"Lerato is still very young, and for her to have a child now would be like a trap that she wouldn't survive and, honestly speaking, I want to marry her someday. I just don't think that she's thinking about the same things at the moment, even the thought of ever getting married has never reached her, so I'll just let the whole thing be and it'll work itself out in the best way there is."

"Whose way is that?"

"The way that things are and have to be."

Lerato got naked with D'nice and to this day Modishi doesn't know and will never know. It has passed beyond being a secret and is forgotten.

Then Molamo too got naked with Modishi's Lerato, more than three times in our haven, because s/he had reasons.

Then, one day, not long after Matome left, it became clear why Lerato got away with all of that. Lerato was play-loving with Modishi and she looked at him in a playful manner and said, "Fuck you, Modishi."

"Don't ever say that again, please."

"Fuck. You. Modishi."

"Lerato, don't ever say that again, ever."

Then she crossed the thin line that she probably thought didn't exist. Not meaning to cross it but just being playful.

"Fuck. You."

She couldn't finish that, Modishi thrashed the hell out of her. He couldn't touch the face or further down at that manly church, but everywhere in between got very badly bruised. If there had been a case brought against him it would have been grievous bodily harm, but there was never a case because, even under pressure from her mother and godmother, she couldn't bring herself to report him.

Modishi showed up at the hospital, just hours after the incident. Molamo, the Zulu-boy and I were the ones who took her there, after much discussion and not knowing what exactly to do, because taking her to hospital meant that eventually Modishi would fry. Because, you see, the hospital is full of female nurses with perpetual man hate, and if you could see what Modishi did to Lerato: one disjoined rib, one broken, as well as first-grade bruises, by his hands only. We couldn't believe it and neither could Lerato.

Molamo looked at him and thought: If he can do that to a woman that he loves, what if it was a man? And he felt his bones leaving him in fear. Then, seeing the fear in Molamo's eyes, Modishi justified himself, "Lerato was wayward, she had to be put back in line."

"What did she do?"

"She was wayward and I couldn't allow her to go astray any more."

That scared Molamo, he was thinking that maybe she had confessed that she gave it to him. Molamo managed to say, "Modishi, you are scaring me and now I can't bear to look at you."

Modishi looked at Lerato, not knowing what to say, not knowing where to start with this apology business, then his tears let themselves out. She put on a hurting smile and gave him her hand, pulling him close. He sat down on the bed and she hugged him and said, "Modishi, I'm sorry and I want you to forgive me in your heart, and we will never talk about this as it never happened. You don't have to say anything about it but you have to forgive me, just forgive me one last time, and give us another chance because I love you too much."

That was it: forgiveness. They forgave each other. Modishi's Lerato and Lerato's Modishi.

Lerato's mother and godmother didn't approve of Modishi after that and they tried to separate the two, but achieved nothing but separating Lerato from themselves. She moved out of the suburb.

Nearly four months after Matome left our haven, Modishi packed up and deserted our haven too. He moved into Lerato's apartment in Illovo. There was an agreement that he would do music part-time and study part-time. Lerato was taking care of all the bills. She had graduated and got a job in Sandton, which she left after three months, moving to another post in Randburg and the last time she ever called me she was settling in at SAA, saying, "I'm settling for now till a better offer comes."

* * *

Modishi sold his land eventually.

Then he moved them out of that expensive, cramped place and got himself and his wife a house in Midrand. The right time had come for her to have a baby; the baby girl, Lerishi, must be one and a half now.

The only time I paid a visit Lerato looked just the same as the Lerato I used to know. She still made me wish some things that you aren't supposed to wish about other men's wives.

Modishi, meanwhile, had gained weight, even though he now had a small gym in the house. He looked like an African politician, with a belly that was forcing itself into existence as if someone had put yeast in his bloodstream. That voice in me said: *That is good living.*

Lerishi. I asked about the unusual name – what it meant. Found out that it was a combination of their names and had no meaning at all except that she was the daughter of Lerato and Modishi. If babies are beautiful then, I thought, she was more than that. But as I watched her father help her walk, trying to have a baby chat with her in baby language, I began to feel empty inside and jealousy started to choke me.

Lerishi took all the love that her father had for her mother. I don't know for sure, but I think Modishi doesn't love Lerato any more, he's only devoted to her now.

When talking about Lerato behind her back, he said, "The woman thinks she is a queen."

But to her face he treated her as if she were a queen.

Then I thought for a moment and realised that trouble was brewing up in paradise, and that made me smile. But with every bad thought, there was a ton of energy that just drained out of me. And, although I had planned to spend the whole afternoon there, I made up some excuse to leave as soon as I could. Father and daughter had to drive me back to Joubert Park.

That was the final straw, and Molamo would say "excuse the cliché" to that, but it was the final straw and it was the last time that I saw Modishi, his Lerato and their daughter Lerishi because, believe me, I don't want to spend my life wishing that bad things happen to other people. It was after visiting Modishi and Lerato that I decided it would be better if I stayed by myself.

* * *

The last time I was talking to Molamo he said that Modishi had been "putting Lerato back in line" too much lately and, as you know, she always forgives him after that.

"Modishi loves Lerato so much that he is going to kill her and then kill himself. I don't even want to think about little Lerishi. One should love things, but that love should outgrow the things eventually. Anyway, let's hope for the best," said Molamo.

Lerato and her Modishi.

Zulu-boy

S'busiso found out that he had the three names, his ticket to the other life.

He called, personally inviting me to his own funeral. How many people do you know that would do that?

"I want you to be there when they are closing the Zulu out."

I took it he was joking.

He said, "I have Aids."

I didn't believe him, people with Aids don't shout it out loud to the world.

"Listen, listen, I have lived a life, one great life for me and I want you to write about it. Write about a Zulu boy who was poor but his happiness superseded all the happiness of the happy people of the world. Write about a Zulu man who said 'I love you' to a prostitute and kissed her."

"You're joking and it's not a good joke at all."

He didn't really have a chance to tell me what he wanted to because I just didn't believe him, but he's gone now, he wasn't joking. I saw a casket with his body inside enter the ground and strong Zulu men cover it with the rich Zululand soil.

He loved Hillbrow. We were all there thinking about Khayalami, but he was there thinking, "I'm living the life." He had reached his Khayalami.

He just disappeared with the Swazi girl. Took all his belongings out of the haven and just disappeared. That was after his collaboration with one of the all-time stars of our music industry, Brenda, and even though the song wasn't that much of a hit the Zulu-boy didn't have any complaints, because, as he said himself, "If it had been a hit, I couldn't walk Hillbrow as a free man. I would have to compromise everything and that would not be a good life."

He told me that when he was working with another fallen star, trying to help the brother recapture the market. I can't say what happened to the project because it never did hit the shelves.

He called Matome: "Satan of a Pedi boy, hope you are enjoying the sex."

"Zulu, what is the occasion?"

"I am on time. I was born on time, lived on time and I am dying on time. That is the occasion: I am on time."

"We are all on time."

"Do you know my mother?"

Of course Matome didn't know his mother.

"She is a big Zulu woman with a big Zulu heart and you are going to see her soon and you will see my sister too."

"I can tell you are enjoying yourself, but can I call you later because right now I'm trying to be on time too."

"You will talk to a ghost, Matome. Anyway, Matome, the living live, the dying die, all on time. Mfana womPedi," and, with that, he cut the call and called Modishi.

He got his voice mail, he left a message: "Mfana womTswana, I'm going to sleep today and you will not see the Zulu tomorrow."

He called D'nice and D'nice answered his phone, saying: "This time, you call me? What is going on? You are getting married?"

"Yes, to death."

"When is the wedding?"

"Tonight, and nothing can separate us, it is divorce-less marriage."

They laugh and D'nice, taking him to be joking, asked: "What's up? You sound high, are you smoking?"

"I'm not high, I have Aids."

"Don't we all have that and it's just that we don't know yet? It's fashion. If you don't have it you aren't living yet and when you start living you will have it somehow."

His voice changed.

"Ja! That I have it doesn't make me inhuman, nor does it make me a fool."

"You are serious?"

Pause.

"I am dying, D."

Pause.

"I don't know what to say to you."

"What can you say to a dying man if you don't know where he's going? All you can do is feel sad for all the things that I will miss when I'm not here."

"What will you miss the most about this earth?"

"Sex."

D'nice managed to laugh.

"You're sick, you know that. To wherever you're going, I will dedicate one to you every night."

The brother called us all, inviting us to his funeral. How many brothers do you know that can do that? There are not that many who can live with pride and die with pride as the brother, the Zulu-boy, did.

The brother is dead but he was there, I guess, and so were Matome, Molamo, Modishi, D'nice and I. It was a reunion in every way. The first reunion we had after the out-of-Hillbrow party and the last one that we ever had, will ever have.

We didn't have much to say to each other. Actually, we tried as much as we could to avoid each other but at least we had that out-of-Hillbrow party.

Molamo

Molamo went to Khayalami just for a visit, to see the other Molamo, and that was that.

In Khayalami he recognised everything that he needed, everything he had been working hard to have.

"Lucifer, let's go visit Tebogo."

He said lucifer because he didn't want to sound like he was begging me to come with him.

I pretended that I hadn't heard him.

"Lucifer, I said that Tebogo has invited us to come to her place."

I shook my head no.

"Why not?"

"She only wants you there, but she didn't want to be obvious so she said that if you can't come alone invite your friends."

"So what are you saying?"

"That she wants you there alone, not with me, because if she had wanted me there she would have invited me too. Enjoy it, but watch it, you might not come back."

She's been waiting for far too long, a voice in me added, and then I said it out loud: "She's been waiting for far too long for you. You might eat things," I joked.

Tebogo wasn't the kind of woman who would have gone to the floor-shift to keep a man and, even if she had, it wouldn't have done him any good as it would have done away with his mind.

"You think that about Tebogo?"

"Yes, she's a woman, isn't she? A whore like all of them?"

He looked at me in a way that he had never looked at me before. For the first time he didn't approve of the fact I'd called Tebogo a whore. In a way, not believing it, I pushed a little more. He'd been calling her a whore forever. Why would he suddenly disapprove today?

"She's a whore like all her kind. Why would she not do what her kind is capable of doing? It's in her blood. It's a natural instinct for her to whore."

Not a good thing to say to a very unhappy man.

"Say that again?"

"A whore is a whore and will remain a whore . . ."

Before I could go on explaining, two hard punches reached this face and I fell on the bed. He took his phone from the charger and walked out of 207 and, for a moment, I couldn't really tell what had happened.

He stopped at the door, wondering to himself: What have I done? He looked back with tears in his eyes, with the knowledge that if it came to it I could trash him so bad that he'd lose a tooth. But I had already forgiven him.

* * *

The other Molamo wasn't there when he got to Khayalami. There was an intercom and a security guard at the main gate and, once he'd passed that, there was another gate, which was already open.

Tebogo looked up at him from behind the sliding door, smiling, thankful that he'd come alone. As he came close, and she stood to open the door, she could see the tears, the resentment, the failure and the anger. He bowed his head, trying hard to put on a smile as the tears pushed themselves out.

She opened her arms wide as she couldn't find anything comforting to say, and he crashed into her arms. Then she lost herself as well and the tears found their way out without permission, with the knowledge that he was finally home to stay.

With tears on their cheeks, she kissed and kissed him. Then she let her hands slide down, unbelted him and helped his jeans down, followed by his underwear. She pulled up her dress, took down her underwear, aptly labelled Triumph, and crowned Molamo with it.

* * *

"You are welcome to stay. This is your home, your property."

Pause.

"You can do with it as you please. You are the man of the house here and this house can't do without you any more."

She said it and meant it.

Molamo closed his eyes, trying to think of something, anything, to say, but he didn't have anything left to say.

She looked at him, then she held him very tight, and whispered, "Lamo, you are mine by destiny and from this day we are married – you are my husband, I'm your wife. I'm Molamo's mother and you are his father; this is his home and we are his parents, because I'm tired of being alone and lonely. Do you agree?"

We make plans every day, we scheme now and then, but things mostly go their way and we have to start scheming and planning some more; but there are those of us that, when they scheme, they twin-scheme, scheme a backup scheme. This is the scheme and, if it doesn't happen, there is the second scheme – they don't wait for the other to fail. Tebogo was one of these.

Tebogo sat on top of Molamo and said, "Open your eyes."

This time she didn't sound like the Tebogo Molamo knew. Her voice had somehow changed and the new tone forced him to open his eyes, fast. There was a gun in her hands and tears dropped at intervals out of her eyes, hitting the gun. He had been shot once, had an idea what a gun could do, and he hated the thing with all his heart.

"Tebogo."

It had been three hours since Molamo had arrived and that was the only thing he had said in those three hours.

"Molamo." Calmly and very sure of herself.

"Tebogo." Scared and very unsure of himself.

"Molamo."

"I'm very sorry."

"I'm very sorry too."

"Don't shoot me."

"Don't want to shoot you. I could never, never hurt you, Molamo."

She paused, looking at him, at the gun, at him again and at the tears dropping on him.

"Molamo, I can't live without you."

This wasn't the first time he'd heard this line, but it was the first time he'd heard it coming out of Tebogo. It scared him and he peed.

"I'm peeing."

"I can't live without you any longer. I can't come and live with you there because I hate it there. I hate Hillbrow. And here: here I love it very, very much, Molamo. But I'm not happy here either. I want you here, to be happy and I want you here, and if I can't have you, I'm better dead."

She turned the gun to her own head.

"Tebogo."

"Lamo."

"Ntebo."

There was a pause. They were looking at each other; scared, shaking.

"Do you want me to live?"

"Yes."

She paused, thinking that he would have something else to say, but he didn't know what to say.

"Want me to be your wife?"

"Yes."

"Lamo."

"Ntebo."

"I want to be your wife. If you ever leave me again, if you ever, ever leave me again, I'm dead. I love you and can't live without you."

She started shaking and crying out loud as the gun fell on the bed, hitting Molamo's head.

"I can't, I can't live without you anymore."

* * *

They didn't notice how much time went by till the other Molamo came in, and shouted, "Ma."

Tebogo tried to cover her naked body, which the other Molamo was used to. He knew its nakedness – he washed in the same bath and slept in the same bed.

"Molamo, when did you come back?"

For a second he was startled by the unusual question, but then he saw his father.

"Oh! Dad!"

"Molamo."

"That's not my name, it's your name."

218

And, with that, he turned and gently closed the door. He was happy. His father and mother were together.

*　*　*

He woke up in the morning, after making up Matome's voice in his head: "I'm waking up."

He opened his eyes, Tebogo was readying herself for work and the other Molamo for school and he gave away a smile that he had been saving for far too long.

"Dad."

"Lamo."

"Will you still be here when I come back?"

"I'm here now and I will be here then."

"Good, because there's something I want you to help me with."

And, for the first time in his whole life Molamo felt he had enjoyed sleeping and there was no need to nap a bit, turn or stretch his bones there and here, there was no need for that. He had rested.

*　*　*

Molamo completely de-havened the haven. He took a chair and sat at the security checkpoint. The security guards weren't there but the make-upped one was; she asked him, "What's your problem?"

"I'm a grown-up. I have a son and he needs me."

She heard it in his voice, that this Molamo wasn't the same as the one she was used to.

"I'm going."

"Where?"

"I'm taking my rightful place and I'm going to play the part – be a man, a father and a husband."

But even as he said it, Molamo felt that it wasn't a very good answer, it felt unfinished, as if there was something missing. Then he realised that he had forgotten to say "excuse the cliché" and he suddenly felt like a stranger to himself.

The thing he feared: the Khayalami he was going to wasn't his place, it was Tebogo's place, and everything in it Tebogo had worked hard for. He looked down at the car keys in his hand. The key ring was a mirror. He turned it carefully, at an angle, and noticed for the first time that there were three pictures in the mirror: his picture with his name, Tebogo's with her name and the other Molamo's with his name. He turned the key ring slowly, letting the light catch it, lost in thought, then he mocked himself: "Rra-baki."

*　*　*

Molamo is still in dream city, somewhere in the northern suburbs, dreaming that dream till its restful end in dream-heaven. The last time I called him, I was asking for some rands that I promised to return, but which, even today, are not returned and will never be returned, believe me on that one.

Tebogo got him and pinned him down. They are having their second-born soon; maybe he is even breathing the city's contaminated air by now. Molamo was going to name him Mogale as a tribute to all that he put Tebogo through; and, to Tebogo, it meant that, after all that she had been through, she was triumphant, she was Mogale.

She was even paying for him to go to that great institution of higher education to finally get the degree that he came to the city to have. She was paying to make him into a good father figure for the other Molamo. He was studying law and, in my opinion, that was high treason to the arts, but I understand, as the Zulu-boy once told him, "With this

220

writing business of yours, lucifer, you are going to die a very poor man. I advise you to stop now, because ours is not a reading nation and reading is a time-consuming exercise. People of long ago had to read because they didn't have satellite television – that is why they had to read."

Revelation

I am the last to leave the place, sorry, the haven. We lived here, and thank you, you were so good to us, thank you very much.

Most of my stuff goes out through the balcony. What I leave behind are all the things that I don't need or that I can do without. A few people see me, but they know that I'm not a thief and that there is no need to report this unusual business, because to them it is usual, it's the Hillbrow way of moving flat. The single bed is the first thing to leave, I claim that it's Matome's and they let it out through the gates without guessing my intention.

Where is the bed now?

Sold to the highest bidder.

I unhook the curtains. They weren't mine. I, we, found them here, but I'm taking them with me. Not as a souvenir: I might need them, wherever I'm going.

We found the double bed here as well, when we first moved in, so I just take the covers off. Modishi loved this bed and he really hated it when some girl had slept in it, leaving her passionate odours behind. He was very stupid, that brother of mine.

I managed to laugh at that thought, and a voice in me asks: *And what about D'nice?*

He had a problem, that one. He could do anything he wanted and that's why he lacked focus. Let me tell you, Jack of all trades is a very confused individual.

The Zulu-boy?

If anything, Hillbrow was his heaven. He found everything he needed here.

Matome?

I look at myself in the mirror, shaking my head, enjoying the reflection for a moment; then I look at the back of the mirror, trying to shake it loose, rocking it from side to side.

Matome had the ability to switch his thinking on and off and there is nothing more remarkable than that.

Molamo?

I think that Molamo was very happy when he was living here, but now all he's doing is fulfilling other people's lives and making them happy because I don't think that he is happy. He will learn to be happy, though.

I take out a knife and start to scrape the rubbers holding the mirror to the wall.

We are taking it, a voice in me says.

I take my time removing the mirror. Then I wrap it in a blanket, strap it in with ropes and then slowly let it descend from the balcony.

Then, finally, I watch my papers going down, taking the same journey that Matome's television took and, as they fall, I remember the thousand pieces that followed that fall, but the papers are still intact, everything is still intact. I still need them.

I group the five keys on the table, taking the key rings. I will need them. Then I close the decaying door very gently for the last time.

We stayed here for too long. We had twelve lockouts and more than twenty-five shutdowns. We were the most troublesome tenants, and the funniest. We once drank R4 200 on the weekend of the nineteenth of August in '96, a 207 record, and we didn't have any money before we started drinking.

The Zulu-boy held three 207 records. Firstly, for keeping a member of the female species here for the longest period. Secondly, for never getting drunk, however hard he drank. And, thirdly, for having more children than any of us here – thirteen, he claimed, but we only ever had proof of seven.

Molamo held one record, for always being the dumper – proven by twenty-five of Molamo's girls that we knew of, of which three were married – and the 207 honour for being the most creative of all.

D'nice held three. One, for being the only one with a degree. A second, for being the funniest drunkard. And a third, for bringing the most beautiful girl into our haven – half-black, half-Indian Jarush. I still maintain that Modishi's Lerato was the most beautiful girl to ever grace our haven, but I was outvoted.

Modishi held only one record: for having one girlfriend all his 207 life.

And Matome held two 207 records, one for having a godlike self-control and the other for being the most business-minded of us all.

I take my last walk past the dead lifts and down the stairs to the first floor; I pass the lifts and then I'm in the stairs. Then I'm on the ground floor. I pause.

Do I have to be that fast? I ask myself.

No, I'm not running away, I'm only moving out and not rushing to get anywhere. I turn and walk back up the stairs, like I'm looking for something, like I forgot something.

Back on the second floor.

This is one of those moments.

I look around; take in the rotting door to 207, the emergency stairs between 207 and 208 that are neglected and rusting. You have to be careful on these stairs: some are already missing and others might just fall under you, and I don't want to think where you would be then. I have never used them, not even once.

I'm tempted to use them now. The temptation to exit that way rises, but I shake my head. No, some risks are just not worth it.

Do an African thing in front of the rotting door, put my hands together and bow my head, in great respect, fear and honour. "It's been an absolute pure pleasure."

Walk slowly down the corridor, my left hand touches the lift doors. Then into the stairs with both my hands touching the walls and I'm on the first floor. I make a slow three-hundred-and-sixty-degree turn with my eyes closed. Down onto the ground floor, push the security door, putting on a smile.

This is the last smile for the landlord's slaves. The security guards are here. Some of them that do business in the dark are here too (sorry, angels of the night), and so is the make-upped one and she reminds me that tomorrow she is going to turn off our power.

"No need to do that any more."

"You guys are the most problematic tenants here."

"Yes, we were, but we were very funny, too."

The annoying security guard mumbles something.

"Talk, baba, say your mind, this is the last time we ever talk."

The make-upped one cuts in with her ever-sweet voice: "Where is Matome?"

"You miss him? I miss him too."

I nearly scare myself to death with that honesty. Then my phone rings: these friends of mine that are here to pick up my stuff.

"Ja!"

"Noko, what's taking you so long?"

"I'm still saying goodbye."

"Yes, goodbye them and let's go."

I give them my hand and we all shake hands and this night angel asks, "Why are you shaking our hands?"

"You are humans, aren't you? Sorry, sweetie, if you think that every-thing has to be paid for. I can even give you a hug for free."

I hug her.

"But why today? That is all I want to understand."

"Yes, why today?"

They are all singing it out now.

"Guess I'm feeling good today. I'm relieved."

They look at me suspiciously and, to make it easier, I take her hand, caress it softly and say, "Had an orgasm with you a million times in my heart."

Lied to her just to make her feel good about herself, and she smiles as everybody laughs.

"What do I say to that: thank you or do it again?"

"Just say it's been a pleasure knowing you."

"It's been a pleasure knowing you."

"Thank you, from me and the boys too. I know they have never said it out loud, but they meant to, from Matome, D'nice, Molamo, Zulu-boy and Modishi, it's been a pleasure."

I give the make-upped one the sixth key.

"I am leaving my key here."

"You must come back with the money or you're not getting the key back."

She says it like she is joking, with a smile, but she is being dead seri-ous.

"I don't need it any more."

I let the door close behind me and take a deep breath.

Last Days

Compared to this place, 207 really was heaven. I'm on the sixth floor out of sixteen in a three-bedroom flat on Wolmarans in Joubert Park. If you thought where I came from was bad, change your mind, there are worse things in this life than what you think you know.

My fiancée came by two days after I moved in. She looked at the place very carefully, then looked at me, from my eyes down to my shoes then back to my eyes. Not that she wanted to look at me, but she wanted me to know that she wasn't playing around, that whatever she was about to say was very serious.

"You are one hell of an artist, I know that, I have seen it in your eyes. Look at me. It's not that I dispute that you are doing what you love, but you have to live."

Then tears started to fall out of her eyes and she just let them run down her cheeks.

"You are thirty-two now and all you have is ideas. Swallow your pride. Don't touch me, please, right now I hate you."

Pause.

"No."

And another pause.

"No, I don't hate you. I hate what you have become and I hate what you are going to be, because I can't live with it."

She paused, thinking that I was going to say something, but there was nothing to say. Then she wiped away her tears, turned and walked out. She stopped at the door and took a look at what she was leaving behind, the debris of what she used to love. Then she softly closed the door.

If you are wherever you are, and you think you are in the worst situation possible, that it can't get any worse, you are wrong. I always thought 207 was very bad, but it was luxury compared to this. I rent this room alone, but, all in all, I have counted more than fifty people who share this flat. The main bedroom is rented by eight females. I can't really tell what their source of income is, just as I can't tell how many men live in the other bedroom. The sitting room is, by day, a sitting room, but it doubles as a bedroom and storeroom by night and I never know how many people sleep there.

207 was a better place. Whoever the landlord was cared a little about that place, and here, he doesn't care at all. Here the lifts are also not working and you'll have to walk to the sixteenth floor. Here there are no cleaners, we are all living in a rubbish dump and paying for the privilege. If the city authorities were playing their role properly this building would be condemned.

I'm living here now.

It is my personal isolation room.

Come in, I am all alone.

Lost my phone in this room, and I lost that and this as well. I am just losing things in this place. Lost everything: my self-respect, my belief, my friends and girlfriends. I am being de-city-ised.

I spend my days in here with thieves that will look me in the eye and smile like they have done nothing to me.

I am in isolation, with my face in my hands.

I stand up, looking at the door, or I just stand and hold the door handle for an hour, and then I'm back to the sponge, face down.

It's like I'm waiting for someone to come and get me out, but whoever it is never comes.

I try to smile, it's been one very great adventure. If there was a re-wind button I would push it right now and start all over again. Not to have it any other way but the very same way.

Pause.

No, I'm lying to myself. I would like to go to Wits and have a degree but . . .

Badbye

I am at Wanderers Street taxi rank.

Someone said to me once, smiling, "The day you die is better than the day you were born."

A voice in me translates: *The day you leave Johannesburg is better than the day you came to Johannesburg.*

But the day I am leaving Johannesburg is a sad day for me.

There is a kwaito song playing in my ears: "The Way Kungakhona". I'm going home and that is the way it is. A tear pushes itself out of my eye and I wipe it away; there is a dam there that is about to burst, but a man doesn't cry.

This adventure will be my life history. When I think about it, it was my life and life itself has no failures or successes, it is just living. It is us who give this life these terms.

Be real, you are a failure, a voice deep in me says.

I admit it to myself. My venture, this adventure in Johannesburg, is a failure. Matome once said that there are people who are just designed to hold you down. Yes, there are, but, you see, I myself took a long shot at an adventure, seeking my fortune in this part of the green earth.

My adventure in Johannesburg has ended. The vow that I took with myself, of driving myself out of Johannesburg, has been broken. I'm still going out like I came in: taking a taxi out.

I don't know much of what I'm going to do at home. There is nothing much to do there. The last time I was there I spent my whole time with bomahlalela, locked in their own isolation rooms. Waiting for the door to open so they could find themselves, they too are a sad black story.

Three taxis take the platform, one after another, get full and leave me here. I say that I am waiting for somebody when the annoying queue-marshal asks.

The noise that people are making.

I can't hear any more.

A tear drops out.

"Why are you going home?" the city asks, not willing to let me go, and I give no answer.

"What are you going to do there?"

*   *   *

I've been here since half-eight and now it's fourteen fifty-two.

Can a goodbye last that long?

I am not thinking any more, my mind froze with the words, "Monna o bolawa ke se a se jelego."

I've been fighting tears since this morning. I now bow my head, I've lost that fight, and look at them drip-dropping onto this paved ground that I came to know as Johannesburg.

I can't remember the last time I cried.

The beginning of something is better than its end. Believe me. I know.

I remember Justice and that painting that he painted fourteen years ago. It comes back into my mind after so many years. It creeps up on me, like it was a hint that I should have taken into consideration as I was going through my life, but I can't get the significance straight even today. Maybe I should have . . . I don't know what. Yes, Matome is smiling and I'm very sad now, with no happy woman by my side.

234

Was that a prophecy? He can't have foreseen my sad end with this city, can he?

Too many thoughts cross my mind, I'm reliving-living fourteen years of hard nothing and always ending up in the future, a future that I have to face, a future which, every time I think about it, turns pitch-black so that I can't see anything, even my big nose.

I am leaving Johannesburg.

Life is never fair, I tell myself, choking to even get into the taxi.

I am leaving all alone on this afternoon.

Glossary and Idioms

bomahlalela (Zulu):   The unemployed brothers, "hlalela" literally means an observer

cheese boys (slang):   Boys from rich families

Chinese radio (slang):   A counterfeit radio

Chinese smile (slang):   A false smile

floor-shift (slang):   Sangoma

four wheeler (slang):   A vehicle

Ga le phirime (Northern Sotho): Literally "It [the sun] doesn't dawn", name given to rat poison

Isando (slang):   The home of South African Breweries

Jah (slang):   Higher being of the Rastafarians

Kgole'setswadi (Northern Sotho): Literally "Far away from parents"

Khayalami (Zulu):   Literally "my home"

komeng (Northern Sotho): Initiation school

Kungakhona (Zulu):   "It is"

Lalelani la (Zulu):   Listen here

lekgosha (slang):   A prostitute

lekhamba (slang):   A mayonnaise jar now used for drinking

lekwerekwere (slang):   A foreigner

lelaenara (slang):   A streetwise person

lengolongolo (slang):   A 750 ml bottle of beer

madoda (Zulu):   Men

mhlolo ka Jesu (Zulu): Miracle of Jesus

mogale (Northern Sotho): A warrior

Molobedu (Northern Sotho): Someone from the Balobedu tribe of the African rain queen

Moshate (Northern Sotho): A king's palace

ntepa (Northern Sotho): Vagina

pilisi (slang):   Drugs

red map:	Blood remains where someone bleeds
red mercury:	A ficticious substance linked to the making of nuclear devices
Rra-baki (slang):	Literally "Mr Suit", meaning a man who came into an already established home, he came in with just his suit
Seven Star (slang):	Knife, Okapi Seven Star
spat (slang):	To impregnate
Titos (slang):	Money, after Tito Mboweni (the governor of the South African Reserve Bank)
TWR:	Technikon Witwatersrand
Valaza (slang):	The big American cars of the 1950s, '60s and '70s

Idioms:

Monna ke nku o llela teng (Northern Sotho idiom):	A man is a sheep, he cries inside.
Monna o bolawa ke se a se jelego (Northern Sotho idiom):	A man is killed by what he eats.

KGEBETLI MOELE was born in Polokwane and raised on a family farm. He has worked in the entertainment industry for most of his life and is currently studying part-time. *Room 207* is his first published novel.